AUDITION

SKYE WARREN

CHAPTER ONE

The novel Oliver Twist shone a light on the plight of poor children who were forced to work in harsh conditions much like a prison. They were fed primarily gruel and soup, only given tea when prescribed by a doctor.

BETHANY

BLINDING LIGHTS. ACHING lungs. Thunderous applause.

The opening show ends the way we rehearsed for weeks, only this time with an audience. My muscles know the movements better than they understand the rest. The prospect of after, of anything outside this stage, makes my breath catch.

We take our bows together, as a single line. The avant-garde dance company doesn't have a strict hierarchy—no corps dancers or prima ballerinas. There's only this show, this moment, which suits me perfectly. No promises. No regrets.

The curtain falls.

Almost to the second, we break formation—a flock of crows startled from the woods. We prance to the dressing room, our bodies made springy by adrenaline. Euphoria clings to our sweat-dampened skin even backstage.

Grins and congratulations all around.

The show is titled *Olivia Twist*, a contemporary retelling with most of the roles gender reversed. Fagin has been reimagined as Fanny, the clever head of a group home for girls. The concept was mine, but the entire show is a team effort.

There's relief, too. The standard ritual of icing swollen joints or wrapping bruised tendons. We hurl our bodies through the air, forcing massive impact through tired joints night after night. We look strong onstage. Behind the curtain we're a jumble of never-healing wounds, held together by silk and spandex and Kinesio tape.

I catch my friend Marlena under my shoulder. Her face is white with pain.

"Ice," she says. "Or better yet—tequila."

I help her limp off the stage. "Don't sell yourself short. You can have both."

A delicate snort. "Not likely. We have to smile and flirt with the old men with big, fat wallets. As if I don't do enough of that at home."

We fall into our creaky chairs in the dressing room. The stage director tosses half-frozen bottles of Ozarka at each of us, and we both pause to gulp. I'm wearing an army-green leotard sewn with rags to highlight my part as the gender-reversed Olivia Twist, while Marlena wears a patchwork greatcoat for her part as Fagin.

I drip some of the cold water into my palm and smooth it across the back of my neck. "You don't have to. At home, I mean. You definitely have to flirt at the opening party."

"My body hurts too much to give up my whirlpool tub or two-thousand-thread-count sheets." Marlena has a sugar daddy who visits her a few times a week for an uncomplicated evening. In exchange he pays for an upscale brownstone once owned by a Hollywood actor, a Bentley and driver to take her to and from practice, and a 401K through his company.

"Does he have any friends?" I ask, though I'm joking—mostly.

"You know I'd find you a sugar daddy if I thought you'd actually accept it. We probably don't even need to. I've seen the way Scott looks at your ass. He has more than enough money to keep both of us."

I choke on a swallow of water. "Marlena."

She giggles. "He may be old, but he knows how to show a girl a good time."

"We'll call that plan B. Besides, I like my apartment." The dance company doesn't pay very much. Less than minimum wage. They get away with it because it's considered a part-time job. We're only paid for the time we perform, even though we practice eight hours a day.

I don't precisely like my apartment, but it's all I can afford.

Marlena rolls her eyes. "Let me know when you get tired of the rat droppings."

For that comment I flick my fingers, spraying her with ice-cold water. She squeals and spills some of her water on my thigh, making me gasp. She thinks I'm too uptight to accept a sugar daddy, like maybe I look down on her. That's not it. I learned early on the risk of belonging to a man. The danger of trusting one.

Being a ballet dancer is a terrible business model. My only commodity is my body, and between injury and age, it depreciates quickly. Still, it's managed to keep me off the streets. It's managed to keep me independent from my brother.

For that I'm grateful.

I remind myself of that as I sit at my bench. We're contractually obligated to attend the ball. Like Marlena said, we should smile and flirt with the rich people who attend. Both the male and female dancers have to. It's what convinces the sponsors to write checks that will fund the next season. Ticket sales don't even cover our tiny paychecks.

Fresh lipstick. Powder. I smooth a hand over my bun, but it's perfectly tight. The truth is that I look composed most of the time. People assume I must feel that way, too. It's an act as surely as I dance on the stage each night. A performance.

I'd love to change into a fresh leotard and shoes, but Rio would complain. They like us sweaty, the stage manager says. It adds to the authenticity. Five hundred rich people of New Orleans will be wearing gowns and tuxedos. Meanwhile I'm damp with sweat and the remains of our impromptu bottled water fight, wearing an army green leotard with bits of frayed fabric forming a ragged tutu.

Chandeliers blind me. The chatter is a physical sensation, like hitting a wall.

Rio hands me two glasses of champagne. "Dunn's on stage left."

My stomach sinks. Trevor Dunn is a real

estate mogul who thinks his corporate sponsorship gives him the right to grope the dancers. Unfortunately he has a particular liking for me. I look around for Marlena, but she's already with Scott Castle. He stands in a black suit with silver-blond hair, a stern expression on his face. They met at one of these events last season, and he hasn't missed one since. He wants the other men to know she's taken. His hand on her ass doesn't leave any ambiguity.

From all the way across the room I hear Trevor's over-hearty laugh. God. He probably wants to become my sugar daddy. The idea makes my throat clench. My eyes burn.

Mamere's voice rumbles through my head. *You come from priestesses and warriors, child. Why you want to take off your clothes and dance for white men?* She's never thought ballet was different from being a stripper. As I approach the drunk men on the left side of the ballroom, the knot in my stomach tightening with every step, it feels like she's right.

It might seem like being onstage, but for me it's completely different. When I perform, my footwork is predetermined, the choreography practiced so well it feels like second nature. This? I try to avoid the boisterous crowd. People jostle me. They bump into me.

They make the champagne slosh against the glasses.

Golden liquid slips over the rim. It spills between my fingers. When I arrive at the group of men, they're caught in the grip of belly laughs—most likely over something lewd or offensive. These are the quintessential frat boys all grown up.

I'm the girl from a family where no one's been to college.

"Bethany," Trevor says with what I suppose is a charming smile on his perfectly tan face. He's aggressively fit, the kind that must take hours in a gym every morning. He's also aggressively styled with slick hair and expensive clothes and a gleaming male manicure. "You looked great tonight. I can pick you out of the lineup every time."

Heat rushes to my face. He can pick me out of a *lineup* because of my skin color. It's not really a commentary on my talent or his skills of observation. "I brought champagne."

Only as the words leave my lips do I realize how strange it is for me to bring a glass only for him when he's standing in a group of other men. It's something a girlfriend would do.

I don't want him to get romantic ideas about me.

"Thanks, sweetheart." He hands me his empty beer stein as if I'm a server.

It would be less humiliating if I weren't half-naked. The leotard that feels so natural onstage seems obscene as I stand here holding a glass smudged with Trevor Dunn's fingerprints.

I'm the high-society equivalent of a Hooter's waitress.

"That must be for me," comes a low voice I remember from my dreams. Green eyes. A face so handsome it belongs on some kind of movie star, not a soldier for hire. A mercenary. He wears his muscles with an ease that Trevor can't match. Those hands have done things that would make society matrons gasp. That body has moved through the darkest places on earth.

"You." My mind supplies only that word: *you, you, you.*

He gives me a cocky half smile that promises a wicked night. It's the smile that could lure Eve out of the garden. He's not Adam. No. He's the serpent with the dark temptation. "Hello, Bethany."

Trevor frowns. "You know her?"

"We've met," Josh says, taking the other

champagne glass from my numb fingers. He takes a gulp before passing the flute to Trevor. He takes the beer stein, too, putting it in the crook of Trevor's suited elbow. That's how he leaves Dunn, holding three glasses, unable to move his arms without spilling. "Be a good pal and walk that over to the bar," Josh says, not taking his eyes off me.

It seems impossible that Trevor would obey. He does. His friends drift away, too.

Then it's only Joshua North standing in front of me.

"Why were you bringing that fucker a drink?"

His harsh tone makes me flinch. Which annoys me. I don't answer to this man. "It's not any of your business who I bring drinks to. What are you doing here?"

"I'm a fan of ballet," he says, his voice bland.

An unladylike snort. "Of course you are."

"What's not to like? Half-naked women onstage for an hour and a half. Doing the splits. Bending over. And those lifts. I swear your partner had his hand right in your—"

"Oh my God, you're worse than Trevor."

"That's his name?"

"You were talking to him."

"Only because I didn't know his name was

Trevor."

My eyes narrow. "Why *are* you here again?"

"To see you, my darling, my love, my northern star."

He's making fun of me, which would be bad enough—worse because my heart skips a beat at the words, eternally hopeful, eternally stupid. Once upon a time I had a crush on this man, even knowing he could never return the feeling. The whole world is a joke to him. A dirty joke. "Fine, don't tell me."

"I could only count the days that we were apart. Desolate. Lonely."

He really is worse than Trevor. At least with Dunn I can slap away his grasping hands. When I get home, it's easy enough to take a shower. Somehow I don't think hot water is going to wash away the sting of Joshua's mocking tone. "Whatever you're doing here, leave me out of it."

"That's going to be tough to do, sweetheart."

"Why's that?"

"Because I'm here to protect you."

JOSH

I REMEMBER THE hunger, the raw scrape in my stomach, the heaviness in my muscles. The name brings it back to me. Years ago, a different Trevor. Trevor Rawley was an equal opportunity elementary school bruiser. He made sure all of us got a turn under his fists. He came at me looking for my lunch money, but like so many other days, I didn't have any. He would have knocked me around a little regardless, but it pissed him off not to get anything.

Well, I could take it.

Dear old Dad taught me how to take a punch.

One day, though, I decided not to.

I looked at Trevor with his clothes that fit and his pudgy stomach from more food than he needed, food I didn't have. The world turned red. He was twice my size, but I fought and kicked and clawed my way to an ugly victory. I carried my tray with cheese sticks and milk in a bag down the line and handed over his five-dollar bill.

Later that day I was called into the principal's office. Apparently Trevor had bruised ribs and a torn cornea. The cops were called.

And at the end of it, I went home—my belly full.

That's all I had to do? Go apeshit. That's the answer. What's the point of holding back? What's the purpose of denial? That was the day I decided to take what I wanted, no matter the cost.

Bethany Lewis is the one exception.

She's the one thing I wanted that I didn't take. Call it a crisis of conscience. Or a moment of stupidity. That's over now. The moment I saw her name on the dossier at North Security I felt the same hunger, the same raw scrape in my stomach. I felt the heaviness in my muscles.

Like I'd fight the whole world to have her.

She manages a frosty silence all the way to the back offices, her chin high, her lips pursed. Naturally it makes my dick hard. That much I remember about her. Everything she does makes my dick hard. She climbs the back stairs, her tight little ass twitching in her leotard and stockings. I definitely shouldn't grab her butt right now. The word *shouldn't* has always been like a dare to me, like a bully challenging me to stand up to him. Which of course I would every time. If it meant bleeding out in the mud behind the playground, I would.

What's the point of holding back? What's the purpose of denial?

The director looks up when she enters. There's no surprise. I told him she would fight the protection. Most people do. Celebrities. Politicians. Accepting that they need protection means accepting that they're unsafe.

The mind will fight that conclusion long and hard.

She'll fight this for other reasons—because I'm the one offering protection.

There was no knock at the door. No demure waiting for permission to enter. Only as she stands in front of the desk does she hesitate. Such a good girl. It's hard for her to assert herself, but she does.

"Mr. Landon," she says, her voice tight. "Did you give this man permission to follow me?"

"The threats—"

"Everyone gets threats."

I lean beside the window, looking out, scanning for suspicious people. "Everyone gets e-mails from shitheads. *You're too fat. Too skinny. I wish you were dead.* Those are the kind of threats other dancers get, right? The world is full of random assholes. Except that's not what yours say."

Her eyes narrow. "He had no right to show them to you."

"Actually he did. They're the property of the ballet company. They were sent here. Which is interesting. I'm sure this person could have sent them to your apartment." Her dark eyes shutter. "Ah, but he tried that. No response. He escalated the game to get your boss involved."

Her jaw works. "I'm sorry about that," she says, addressing the director. "I didn't mean to disrupt the dance company. If I need to resign my position, I can do that."

Alarm fills his eyes. He's looking at her with more than an employer's interest. "Of course not, Bethany. Don't even say that. I'm only concerned about your safety. You're my responsibility."

A subtle tightening of her lips. "I'm my own responsibility."

The director manages to look hurt, which makes me wonder how far he's pushed his interest. Would he fuck a ballerina who worked for him? Of course he would. Would Bethany let him fuck her in order to be the good, dutiful dancer? That hungry brown gaze sweeps over her body. Too desperate. He hasn't had her yet. It's those damn ethics that get men in trouble. He didn't want to overstep. My brothers have that shit, too. Me? I'm fresh out. I will step all over her lithe little body, framed so prettily in spandex.

"Bethany." His voice becomes coaxing. "You've only been with us for one season. What would happen if you leave now? You have so much more to learn. I have so much more to teach you."

Christ. Bethany's danced with the world-class

touring company Cirque du Monde. She's been on a global tour with the violin prodigy Samantha Brooks. She's a thousand miles above this rinky dink dance joint, a thousand miles above this guy, who only has the job because he flunked out of his MFA with his best friend, who inherited a shit ton of money. They started the avant garde dance company to *challenge the institution,* which is ironic considering they're white men in the one percent.

I pull up the photograph on my phone. A typed letter on the letterhead of a fifty-year-old hotel in lower New Orleans. They could tell me nothing about any possible-stalker guests. I've already tried that angle. "'Dear Bethany,'" I read aloud. "'Why don't you look at me? I'm waiting for you. I've been waiting a long time.'"

"Personal correspondence," she says with the same good effort in the face of the same sheer futility. "That's my personal correspondence."

This woman will never stop fighting. It's the truly twisted part of me that finds her a turn-on. I don't want her surrender. "It's evidence for when your body turns up in a dumpster."

Anger flashes through her dark eyes. It would be more comforting if it weren't also accompanied by panic. "You don't know that. You don't know anything."

I swipe right a few times to the last letter. "'Don't make me come find you. It would only add interest to the debt. I wouldn't have a choice, and I don't want you hurt.'"

She looks away. "Everyone gets threats."

"Not everyone has an old acquaintance wanted by the CIA."

"Mr. North says your brother is some kind of criminal," the director says, standing as if to approach her. The concerned look on his face disguises the concern for the reputation of the dance company, which is what he showed when she wasn't in the room.

Even with the desk between them, she tenses.

She doesn't want to be touched right now. She's always been formal, always held herself in a way that politely invites men not to fuck with her, but the gate is extra high right now. The letter has her scared. Which means there's no goddamn way I'm leaving this office without protecting her.

I'm the only one allowed to scare her.

Landon reaches for her. One arm around her shoulder. I don't launch myself at him, though it's a close thing. She tenses. "We should call the cops," he says. "You said no to that, and I respected your wishes, but we can't ignore this."

"*Auribus teneo lupum,*" I say. "Explain it to your boss, so he understands the proverb. So he understands the situation you're in."

She glares at me. "It doesn't mean anything."

"Holding a wolf by the ears. That's the literal translation from Latin. It's dangerous to do nothing, because you're close enough to get bitten. But it's also dangerous to do *something*, because that means letting go of the wolf. Basically it means you're screwed either way."

"You don't have to face this alone," the fuck-face director says, running his hand down her arm.

"So true." I gently lead Bethany away, sending a quick slice to the pressure point on Fuckface's wrist. He yelps and curls his hand close. *Oops.* "North Security has quite a bit of experience holding wolves by various body parts. We'll keep you safe."

She pushes away from me, from both of us. "Maybe you didn't understand. I'm not hiring you." She glances at Fuckface, who's still cradling his hand like a baby bird. "If you don't want me to resign, I'll fulfill my contract here—but you can't make me accept this security. If you're really concerned about this, and about the other dancers, you can hire general security for the theater."

"You want to rent a cop? I knew you would make this difficult."

"I'm not sorry," she says, her eyes shooting fire.

"Neither am I. It's hotter when you fight me."

"That's highly unprofessional," Fuckface says, glaring at me.

"I'm only saying what we're both thinking." I acknowledge the lithe body wrapped in leotard and tights, my gaze meandering all the way down to her worn ballet shoes. On the outside they look merely frayed. On the inside, it's another story. I imagine she's bruised, maybe bleeding. No doubt there's tape to hold her feet together. The life of a professional athlete isn't pretty. Much like that of a professional soldier. "I'm not opposed to double-teaming on principle, but when it comes to this particular woman, I think I'd prefer to have her all to myself."

Bethany draws herself up. The effect is that of a queen. She could be wearing rags and chains around her ankles. Actually, the leotard and ballet shoes serve the same purpose. They don't diminish her. They only emphasize her inherent dignity. It can't be touched, not even by two assholes fighting over her. "Mr. Landon, I'll see you at practice tomorrow. As for you, Mr. North, I don't expect to see you again. It hasn't been a pleasure. Goodbye."

CHAPTER TWO

Author Charles Dickens was only 12 when his father was imprisoned for debt. Young Charles had to leave school and work in a boot-blacking factory to help his family survive.

BETHANY

MY COAT IS two sizes too large. The pockets are torn out. There's something questionable smudged across the back, but it doesn't matter. No—it's better this way. The coat, the boots, the earbuds that don't play any music. All of it's armor for the train. I keep my eyes down, my chin up. The cars jolt forward. And stop. Forward. And stop. We let our bodies lean into the movement with practiced precision, hundreds of people swaying so that we don't have to touch. It's sort of a dance. A dance of survival. The French Quarter is notorious for being dangerous, but I learned to put my guard up well before I moved here. The streets of New Orleans taught me that from a young age. The earphones and heavy burlap messenger bag are my shields. They help me become invisible. New Orleans taught me that, too.

Mist coats me as I emerge from the tunnel. A smoke shop. Cell phone repair. Knockoff purses. Every store sleeps, the gates rolled down to the concrete, as if even the building needs to ward away the chill. I pull my coat tight. The Chinese restaurant is officially closed, but yellow light presses against the window. Thousands of dollars change hands every night in illegal gambling— mah-jongg with high stakes. I skirt the building to the fire escape. Metal groans from the wind. It screams when anyone actually climbs the stairs. Cold whispers through my gloves. On the third floor the scent of charred meat makes me cough. I can't actually blame my neighbor. Decades ago some enterprising landlord split up the apartment into two parts. I'm lucky enough to have the tiny kitchen. The elderly man next door makes do with a microwave inside and a bucket grill outside the window. Burgers, hot dogs, bacon. All of it cooks a foot away from my apartment. I duck through the bent casing and land lightly in the middle of my space. One hundred and twenty feet that belong to me. I pull the bag over my head and toss it onto the bed—and shriek when the bed catches it. A shadow separates from the dark blanket. "Nice place you got here," says a familiar taunting voice. "I made myself at home. I'm sure you don't mind."

"Of course I mind." My heart pounds loud enough to drown out my words. "This is my apartment. What are you doing here? How did you get in?"

Josh stands and circles me, forcing me to turn and face him. "The same way you did. The same way any rapist or murderer can get in if he wants to. Why the actual fuck do you leave the window open?"

"Because I'm directly over the ovens. If I leave them closed, the place basically cooks all day."

"I suppose it wouldn't do me any good to ask why you rented this shit box."

"I can afford it," I say, my voice sharp. I'm not in the habit of explaining myself. I worked hard to make sure no man could demand answers of me, but Josh has me spooked. How the hell did he beat me here from the theater? He's still wearing his tux, which looks even crisper in the backdrop of my crappy apartment. "Not that it's any of your business. Besides, there's nothing here to steal."

Dark green eyes flicker. "There's you. You're the most valuable thing in the apartment. The most valuable thing in the whole fucking city."

My cheeks warm. How strange to get a compliment from the man who insults me at every turn. Then again, maybe he didn't mean it as a compliment.

He spoke with tight-lipped anger. With derision.

I turn away so he can't see my expression. There's nowhere to go. One hundred and twenty feet have shrunk to the size of my body. A worn bookshelf serves as my closet. A countertop and small oven line the other side of the room. Stockings and leotards hang from the cabinet knobs, drying after I washed them in the sink. My panties hang from a row of hooks. Humiliation squeezes my chest. Hot tears burn my eyes. I refuse to cry in front of him. There's a washateria in the building next door, but it's easier to wash my clothes by hand in the sink. So what if I live in a crappy apartment? He has no right to judge me. He has no right to be here.

"I did wonder about the bathroom," he says, and I jump. He's not on the bed any longer. He's standing behind me. So quiet. So agile. I work with professional athletes every day, but I know when they move. He's some other creature—made of shadows and fury. "Do you climb onto the counter and piss into the sink? Do you lean your pretty little ass outside the window and shit onto the alley?"

Embarrassment mixed with a complete lack of power. It's like I'm back in elementary school. Boys would pick on me. They'd yank my braids and toss my lunch in the dirt. *It's because they like you,* my mother said. I didn't want them to like me. Still don't.

Well, I'm not in elementary school anymore. "Leave or I'll call the cops."

A tsking sound. "I don't think your landlord would like that."

No, he would probably kick me out. "I despise you."

"Was it the pissing comment? I think it would be hot, if it helps."

"There's a bathroom in the hallway." It's not exactly a hallway. The bathroom had been part of the apartment when it took the whole floor. Now it's shared between the tenants. For the most part we manage to avoid eye contact. For the most part I pretend I don't see a grown man wearing only a long T-shirt shuffle in to use the toilet while I shower. "Most nights I shower at the company, anyway."

Josh moves past me. I manage to squirm out of the way, but I still feel the heat of his chest against my arm. He opens the door. I don't have to look to know what he's seeing. A clear view into the bathroom with its cracked tile and yellow liner. The smell of mold and cigarette smoke. "Christ," he says. "I've seen barracks more comfortable than this. Do you have any specific sins you're trying to repent or do you just like wearing a goddamn hair shirt on principle?"

His words hit too close to home. "I don't understand why Landon even called you. There are hundreds of security companies. Like the one that manages the theater. How did he have your number?"

He picks up a book—a history of ballet with a torn lavender cover I got from the library's fifty-cent sale. "Ah, that. It's possible Landon was under the impression I was contracted as your personal security. I visited when you first joined the company to introduce myself."

A wild, incredulous laugh bubbles out of me. We're standing in what's basically a closet that I call my apartment. The idea that I would be able to afford security is crazy. Abruptly my laughter dies. Money. The reason I got into this mess. The root of every bad thing in my life.

And this man—he's no better. A mercenary. A paid soldier. He does violence to make his dollars, and the fact that he has so very many of them, the fact that he's a wealthy man, doesn't make it better.

"Why on earth would you do that?"

"I could say that Samantha asked me to make sure you were protected. Which she did." He peeks inside a rusted tin box, which contains ticket stubs from most of my performances, including the ones I did with Samantha Brooks, the incredible violin prodigy. "The truth is I flew in before she called me."

"You've been *stalking* me."

"After the events of the tour, someone had to look out for you."

Samantha became a target from people trying to keep treason under wraps. We were on tour together when everything came to a head. Shots were fired in the middle of a concert. Secrets exploded onto the newspapers. It was a scary time. Scary enough that I came back to the States. Scary enough that my dancing partner, Romeo, slipped into obscurity. I thought it would be anonymous enough, being one of fifty members of a corps de ballet. How did Terrance even find out I was in

New Orleans? "You should go back and tell Samantha I'm fine. She shouldn't be worrying about me in her condition."

"What condition? Being pregnant? She's a goddamn picture of good health. Basically glowing. And her tits look amazing. If she gets any more healthy, Liam's going to have to fuck her at the dinner table instead of waiting until dessert to drag her upstairs."

I make a face. "Do you have to be so terrible all the time?"

"Me? Terrible? I'm shocked." He puts a hand over his heart. "Wounded."

"You're an asshole."

He gives me a stately bow. "Yes, but I'm an asshole who's going to keep you alive."

"No, you're not."

The tarot deck sits on my nightstand, the edges worn, one card flipped over from my morning pull. He taps the top with his forefinger. "What's this? Magic spells?"

"It's not magic," I say, even though my mamere would pinch my arm if she heard me.

He picks up the lone card facing up. The moon. I pulled it this morning before the final performance. It symbolizes intuition and femininity. It signifies the pattern that weaves moments into time. I don't believe the cards tell the future, but they carry a quiet significance. It would be impossible for me to hear Mamere give readings for hours every day without feeling something for the deck.

Green eyes spark with mischief. "Are you going to read my palm?"

"Definitely not."

"Come now." He holds out his hand. "If you know something, you have to tell me."

This is my chance to get back at him, to repay even two percent of the teasing and mocking he gives me. That's the only reason I take the warm weight of his hand in mine. That's the only reason I pull him close enough to see—not because I want to touch him. Coarse hair and callused skin. Muscle and tendon. Joshua North always seemed larger than life. The effect should fade up close. Instead he looms even larger. He's a mythical creature. Hercules, half immortal, doomed to live through endless fights, to feel the pain and suffering in each and every one.

So much strength in him. He could probably climb a mountain with his bare hands. Or snap my neck in half. Instead he offers himself up to me. *Auribus teneo lupum.* To hold a wolf by the ears. That's what I'm doing with him. It's dangerous to do nothing, because you're close enough to get bitten. It's dangerous to do something, because that means letting go of the wolf.

Basically I'm screwed either way.

For some reason the thought gives me courage. If I'm going to get bitten either way, I want to pet this particular wolf. I stroke my finger across the middle of his palm. The faintest sound—his breath catching. I'm not powerless here. Heavy callouses across his thumb and forefinger, along the side of his hand, the way a musician might have after years of practice with a stringed instrument. He doesn't make music, though. He makes violence. These are made from the kick of a gun. From practicing again and again. From using it in combat. I absolutely should not find that exciting. It's some primordial part of me that does, the primitive woman who understands this man can protect and provide.

I stroke down the length of his lifeline. "Long. Deep. You'll live a long time."

"If you're going to curse me, couldn't you do it with locusts instead?"

Too intimate. His hand feels abruptly intimate, as if I'm cradling some more sensitive part of him—his heart, maybe. "It's not a curse."

"For someone who's been trying to die his whole life, it is."

I turn our hands so that he's holding mine. My palm is up. I push his thumb across my lifeline. "Short," I tell him. "It doesn't always mean you'll die early. It could mean struggle or illness. It could mean nothing, but my mamere always told me to live while I could."

"What a load of bullshit," he murmurs, and I realize how close we're standing. I can feel his breath on my forehead. His thumb presses over my lifeline, as if he can smudge away the promise it holds. "No wonder you're always so damn serious."

I don't always agree with things Mamere says. Sometimes I even resent them, but it's different when I do it. Hearing him insult us raises my hackles. "Excuse me for wanting to live."

"Then you'll let me protect you."

Somewhere behind me there was a lure and a hook. Now I'm already out of the water. Because of course he's right. If I'm so determined to stay alive, then I should take every precaution.

"I'll keep the window closed."

"Oh, good. No murderer shark has ever gotten past one of those."

I throw up my hands, breaking contact with

him. "What do you suggest? Do you want to sleep out on the fire escape?"

"As tempting as the offer is, I have a better idea. You're coming with me."

"This is my apartment."

"This is a rat-infested firetrap of a building that should be condemned. I wouldn't leave you here even if you weren't in danger. You're coming even if I have to carry you out."

There's the expected annoyance at his high-handed manner, but even more than that, there's relief. It rushes over me in a heady elixir. I'm drunk on it. I don't like boiling over the restaurant's oven when I'm trying to sleep. I don't like averting my eyes when strangers use the bathroom while I shower. A dancer in the corps de ballet doesn't make very much money. Living in New Orleans isn't cheap. And some of what I make goes to mamere. It would be so easy to rely on this man, such sweet relief to sink into that quicksand once again.

CHAPTER THREE

Ballet originated in Italy in the 15th century. At the time, it was illegal for women to dance in public, so they couldn't join the ballet.

JOSH, FIVE YEARS EARLIER

THERE'S A DISTINCTIVE sound to the human body on impact.

Someone must be fighting inside the warehouse. Not surprising, considering it's owned by Caleb Lewis. Then again, there are no sounds of pain. No grunts of exertion. The sounds I do hear, the scuffs and the thuds, are almost rhythmic. Training, then. A thug with a makeshift punching bag.

Metal glints off the warehouse. Cajun spices saturate the humid air. The community has done a decent job of recreating their Louisiana origin after Hurricane Katrina drove them out. Unfortunately the coast is a great deal more porous over the Texas state line. That means easier access in the Gulf to drugs and guns and human cargo. Caleb might only have been a small-time criminal, had Mother Nature not decimated his home. Is he dealing with Russia? North Korea? Either way he's in way over his head. Only a matter of time before he winds up shot in the back. I can join him or I can snitch on him. Not exactly great choices.

I'm doing a little reconnaissance on his properties.

I open the door, expecting to see a couple of rough-hewn bastards fighting or training. They might even take a swing at me. We're all a bunch of army bastards, more comfortable using our fists than our words.

Instead I'm struck by the sight of a body in motion, but not in violence.

She's dancing. Grace. Strength. And completely inappropriate to this place—desire. It's nothing so base as tits and ass, though I'm sure hers are lovely. No, it's the sweep of her calf and the indent at her waist. The lift of her chin.

I could not be more shocked if I had been punched. Or shot.

It feels a little bit like being dunked in lava, watching her dance. I'm immobile in the doorframe of the warehouse. My sanity is one step behind me, utterly gone. I'm seeing visions. She can't be real. I don't even want her to be real. This kind of beauty doesn't belong in the goddamn gutter. A pale pink leotard against the dinge-dark hollow. Satin ballet shoes pushing into the dirt. Slowly, very slowly, my sluggish mind searches the perimeter. Alone. We're alone. If anyone had wanted to shoot me, they'd have had plenty of time. An eternity while I'd been staring.

Her spin slows, like a top that's run out of momentum. Dark eyes meet mine. Surprise. A flash of something else—anger. She drops to flat feet. No longer a goddess, a blur. She becomes a woman. "No," she says. Then again, "No," with such force I glance behind me in case someone's charging at her wielding a knife. The shipyard is empty. It's only my company she's objecting to.

Well, you can't fault her for taste.

"Normally I have to say something for women to hate me," I say, strolling into the warehouse, pretending my heart doesn't thud at the sight of her lithe body. Pretending my cock isn't a breath away from rock-hard. "I have to say something about their tits or their ass."

Her eyes narrow, but she doesn't seem partic- ularly shocked by my crude language. No, she wouldn't be. Not in this place. She would have heard much worse. "I told him no more guards."

"You told who?"

"Who else?" she says. "Your boss."

My boss? I work for the US government. My job is to drive around godforsaken deserts and pray I don't get blown up by a bomb buried underground. If I play my cards right, I might move into special operations. That's what was implied before I went on leave. *Go along with what Caleb Lewis offers. Collect information. Report back.*

It's a chance to be somewhere other than the bottom rung. Maybe the only chance I'll ever get. Which means I have no business being interested in this girl. She probably isn't even eighteen. "My boss," I repeat, my voice flat.

"Isn't that why you're here? To guard me?"

"Why don't we do this—you dance again. I'll stand here, but if anyone attacks you, I'll just let them have at it. No bodyguards for you."

She's not amused. "The guards aren't there to protect me. You're here to keep me in the warehouse or keep me at home. Make sure I don't wander away. Make sure I don't talk to anyone."

"You're talking to me."

"You tell Caleb we had a deal. And it doesn't include some—" Her narrowed gaze sweeps down my body, as if she's only now noticed that I have a body. "Some overmuscled asshole on steroids."

I put my hand over my chest. "Direct hit. I'm wounded you think I'd resort to steroids. These muscles were earned the old-fashioned way, thank you very much."

She snorts, which somehow sounds feminine and delicate. "I'm sure you do much worse things than steroids. And there is no way, absolutely no way, that you're going to be my new guard, so tell Caleb he can forget it."

"Would it put your mind at ease to know he didn't send me?" Though I'm curious how he's connected to her. We enlisted at the same time. Went through basic at the same time. We've never been close, really. When we both had leave, I was surprised he offered for me to hang out with him in New Orleans. I accepted because I have nowhere else to go. At the time I had no idea that I'd be approached by some special department to gather intel for them. Doesn't take a genius to figure out Caleb's into some bad shit.

"Right," she says, unconvinced. "So you're standing in the one warehouse that doesn't contain anything illegal because…?"

"Total coincidence. I was looking for the illegal stuff." Which means I have no business staying to chat with this woman, no matter how compelling she looks with that notch between her eyebrows. She looks goddamn fierce. "Honestly."

A roll of her eyes. "Tell my brother he doesn't need to waste time and energy watching me. I'm staying out of trouble."

Her brother. Jesus. If she's Caleb Lewis's sister, then she's not staying in trouble. It won't be a clean shot that brings him down. It'll be a grenade launcher that hits him—metaphorically speaking. Or literally speaking. Everyone in his vicinity will end up in jail or dead. That's inevitable.

And she's right here.

Don't fucking feel bad for her. For all I know she knows all about her brother's misdeeds. She might even participate in them. She could be his right-hand man.

I don't want to feel bad for her, but I can't control the heavy beat of my heart. She shouldn't be in this dump. She shouldn't be left unguarded. I know better than to let a pretty face or a tight ass make me vulnerable, but I can't help thinking she wouldn't do that. As if her dancing has shown me a window to her soul. *You're a dumb motherfucker, North.*

"You'll have to tell him yourself," I say, taking

a large step forward. Circling her. Forcing her to turn to face me. "I'm not working for him. I'm here on leave. He invited me to come drink and fuck around for a couple weeks."

Her dark eyes shutter. "You're in the army with him?"

"Yeah."

"Say no to whatever he offers you."

What exactly will he offer me?

Some kind of job, that much I know. Something illegal.

I'm tempted to grab the next flight out of Louisiana right now. I don't want to become a snitch, not really, but I have no loyalty to Caleb. The fact that this girl wants to protect me, that she wants to warn me, when she doesn't even know me, turns my stomach to stone. Her feline grace makes me hard. The faint scent of lavender makes me hard. In other words I'm two seconds away from pushing her down into the dirt and fucking her. I could make her like it. Judging from the way her breasts rise and fall in rapid rhythm, she already does.

"What do you think he's going to offer me?"

"Nothing good."

"No? I thought you might want a partner for your lovely ballet studio." I peer into the dusty corners. A few broken shipping pallets. Some flattened boxes. Quite a few scurrying shadows. The richest man in fifty square miles, and his sister practices ballet in a goddamn hovel. How many AK-47s did he have to sell to afford this prime piece of real estate? The least he could do is spring for some air-conditioning.

"Where I practice is none of your business."

"And the business of anyone who walks in here."

"I thought you worked for Caleb." She makes a face. "I'm still not sure you don't."

"A bit of hired muscle, that's what you thought. A bouncer at his nightclub of ammunition and white powder. I don't think he'd like to hire me. I don't take orders very well. Besides, if I got my paycheck from Caleb Lewis, I wouldn't be able to do this to his sister." It's meant to be a threat. To make her flinch. She'll put her fists up. She'll fight me. I loom over her, threatening. If I'm half the thug she thinks I am, she should be wary. In fact I'm worse. Instead her head tilts up. Her dark eyes dare me. I've never turned down a fucking dare.

I have a million graphic images of her in my head. The ways I'll bend that flexible body. The hard fuck I'd give her up against the burning hot wall of the tin box we're in. It's coarse and disrespectful. There isn't a sweet bone in my fucking body, but somehow my lips meet hers. It's a kiss, more innocent than anything I've ever done before—more terrifying, too. She's warm beneath my lips. Pliant. I brush against her slightly, savoring the tremor in her body, the cool rush of her sharp inhale.

"We shouldn't," she says, her Louisiana accent think as sorghum. Even if I hadn't known where she came from, by virtue of her brother's origins, I would recognize the distinctive lilt.

"Of course we should." My voice comes out thick and low. Arousal makes me rougher, usually. Enough that I can slap a woman's ass and have her begging for more. I slip my hand behind her neck, as gentle as if she's made of spun sugar. I can't break her. I can't let her crack. "We're alive, aren't we?" A kiss to her bottom lip, soft enough to make my eyes burn. So goddamn sweet. "You and I, we're surrounded by violence. Surrounded by death. Both of us hurting people just to survive, but this isn't hurting anyone." I kiss the corner of her mouth. There's a shudder through her body. Then she kisses me back—an urgent, artless press of her lips against mine. It's innocence and hope and a painful stab in my chest.

I lied before. It's hurting me, how tender I feel toward this stranger. It's torture.

"What the fuck is going on here?"

Caleb Lewis stands in the doorway. The man I came here to meet. The man I came here to kill. This woman's brother. She moves her body in front of me—*protecting me.* Jesus. When's the last time someone protected me? Not since I was a dumb kid, and my brother took our father's punch meant for me. Then he grew up and enlisted, and I learned how to fend for myself.

There is nothing this slender slip of a woman could do to defend me against her drug lord brother. Nothing I would let her do, but the idea that she'd try to protect me makes my throat burn.

I step around her, approaching Caleb with a cocky smile. It helps to have people underestimate you. "There you are. I figured I'd have a taste of this fine piece since you made me wait."

He scowls. "That's my little sister, you fuck-er."

How could I have known? my expression says, hands raised in helpless amusement. *I'm the kind of dirtbag who makes a pass at every woman, who doesn't take no for an answer. Exactly the kind of bastard you do business with.* "Sorry, man. I thought she was fair game."

There's nothing fair about this woman. She's threatening. Not with guns and knives. I know how to defend against that. She's dangerous because she makes me feel things.

That's what'll get you killed on a job—distraction.

Caleb Lewis frowns. He doesn't look much like his sister. They have the same coloring, but her features are delicate while his are rough. Her eyes are guileless while his are full of shadows. "I'll give you the tour I promised, but you stay the fuck away from Bethany."

I glance back at the woman who's already dipped into a graceful plié, her face in profile. Bethany. That's her name. The woman who turned my fucking world upside down.

CHAPTER FOUR

A professional ballerina wears out 100 to 120 pairs of pointe shoes in a season.

BETHANY, PRESENT TIME

THE TEMPTATION OVERWHELMS me. It's enough to steal my breath, to weaken my muscles. How easy would it be to put myself into this man's keeping? Whatever else he is, he's strong enough to protect me from harm. Except I know what else he is—mercenary. Pretty much heartless. He would protect me for a price far too high.

I'm still paying for the last time I let him help.

"I have to pee."

He blinks, his green eyes startled. For once I've managed to surprise this man. He's worried about threatening letters, not something mundane. Like bathroom breaks. "You do," he repeats, his voice flat.

I push aside my bulky jacket, its size more for

the train than the weather, revealing my performance clothes underneath. "I dressed for the show six hours ago and couldn't change after because of the ball. Kind of hard to go with a leotard and tights."

An athlete doesn't blush about such basic body functions. That's what I tell myself as my cheeks turn hot. His low laugh makes it worse. "Then go, sweetheart. I'm not stopping you."

"And I have to change," I add, grabbing jeans and a T-shirt from the stack of clean clothes on the shelf. I shove them into my messenger bag. It's not that strange to bring a bag into a shared restroom. I keep my shampoo and bodywash in a caddy for easy transport. Anything left on the thin shower shelf ends up taken anyway. So Josh has no reason to object when I open the door to my apartment and cross the small hall to the bathroom, still fully dressed in coat and shoes.

I close the door behind me, staring blindly at the window that's perpetually cracked open. Large enough for a body to fit through. Barely. I'll make it work. After I pee, because I really do have to go. I try not to think about how long Josh will wait for me before he realizes I'm gone.

You're coming even if I have to carry you out.

Joshua North isn't a man who makes idle

threats. I figured that out a long time ago. As tempting as it is to imagine that he represents safety, I know better. There's no safety—not in the tiny Toulouse or the rebuilt New Orleans. Not in the whole world. There's no safety, but I'm after something else. Redemption.

The chance to breathe without this terrible weight on my chest.

I change my clothes without much fanfare. My muscles have tightened up because I didn't do my usual cooldown stretching routine, but there's no time for that. Instead I reach up, high enough that my fingertips brush the popcorn-textured ceiling. That will have to be good enough. Next I crank the metal handle until the window's as wide as it can get.

This is basic acrobatics. Pretend these are bars in a gym. This is part of a dance routine.

I hook my fingertips over the tile edge and pull. Then I'm pushing through the space the same way someone dives into water, arms first, holding my breath. The textured glass presses against my breasts. I wriggle against it harder and gain an inch. Then two. It's easier through my waist, but my hips are the hard part. No amount of sucking in my breath will make them smaller. In the end there's a heavy pain through my side.

Enough that I'll be bruised come tomorrow.

There's a two-story drop onto the awning below. Another fifteen feet to the floor. *You're an acrobat. Be light and quick and strong.* The voice sounds like my grandmother, with her smoker's rasp and thick accent. I study the jumps. One wrong move and I break my arm. Or worse.

My heartbeat slows. My focus narrows. It's the exact same thing that happens when I'm about to perform. *It's the same thing that happens when you see Joshua North.* That one doesn't sound like my grandmother. It sounds like me.

I leap from the window, and I know the angle's right, I feel it from the moment my foot leaves the brick—until my messenger bag catches on the window's ledge. I'm yanked back. Not light or quick or strong. My body lands hard against the building. *Thud.* Then I'm slipping and sliding down the awning. There's the sound of a tear. Then I land hard on the ground. Not my most graceful maneuver, but not bad considering I'm holding an uneven weight.

Without pausing to see if anyone saw me, I set off briskly in the direction of the train. Once I make it on, I can go anywhere. Such as the stately brownstone where Marlena lives. The good news is that it isn't listed under her name. Which means Josh won't be able to find me there.

I only hope Scott Castle doesn't read too much into my late night arrival.

A threesome is really not in the cards.

JOSH, PRESENT TIME

I GREW UP in a town too small to appear on most maps. It was the kind of place where everyone knew everyone else's business. Which means everyone knew that the North boys were wild animals. The single-wide that groaned every time a brisk wind ran through, the field thick with burs and trash—that was our forest. We ran and fought and grew like goddamn weeds. Didn't matter that there was hardly ever food in the pantry. We turned big and strong anyway.

My brother left to join the army as soon as he could. I stuck around as long as legally required until I could do the same. When I took the entrance exam at the high school recruitment office, they put me into a special program. Officially the title on my pay stub says *Information Analyst*. I'm told there's even a cubicle somewhere in an office building with my name on it. The more correct name for what I do is *operative*. I go to whatever country good old

Uncle Sam wants me to go. I find out whatever he wants me to find. Which means it doesn't take me very long to find Scott Castle's love nest.

I'm waiting outside when the dawn breaks across the steeples and gates that make up NOLA's horizon. A century of superstition and voodoo hasn't kept the city safe. There've been outbreaks and fires and floods. It's beautiful even in its wounded state.

Much like the woman who emerges from the front door.

My phone vibrates. "North."

Liam's on the other end of the line. "Found her?"

"She won't be happy to see me."

"Don't fuck it up." My brother's become way too fucking confident after making things work with the woman he loves. As if he didn't fuck things up with her a million times. He doesn't deserve Samantha any more than I deserve Bethany, but that's the thing about women—they want what's not good for them. It's the only reason the human race has perpetuated this long.

The door opens, and two women step out. Marlena has a mass of strawberry-blonde curls that catch on the wind. In contrast Bethany has smoothed her dark hair back into a bun. She always looks so put together. I wonder if she knows it makes me want to mess her up.

Bethany spots me first. I notice the break in her stride even though she keeps walking. I sling myself into step beside them, startling a cry from Marlena. Her eyes widen as she takes me in. What must I look like? I've had no sleep, but I could go for another eight hours before needing a break. That comes from the military. I'm wearing a black T-shirt and tactical pants. I don't go for the suits that Liam and the other close security people have to wear, not if I can help it.

"You know what?" Marlena says, a sly expression on her elfin face. "I don't think I'm actually in the mood to walk. I'll take the Bentley. Meet you there, Bethany."

Bethany shoots daggers at her with her eyes but stays on the sidewalk with me as her friend leaves. "You scared her off," she tells me, accusatory.

"She wants to play matchmaker." I hold up a white bag with a green stamp.

Her hands go to her hips. "A peace offering?"

"Nah, I thought I might get hungry."

She grabs for the bag, but I hold it out of reach. "Say you're sorry."

"Sorry for what?"

"'I'm sorry for making you traipse all over the goddamn city looking for me, when all you were trying to do is protect me, Joshua.'"

"You've never traipsed anywhere in your life."

I shrug and start walking toward the theater. It's only a few minutes away from the brownstone. "Suit yourself. I'm hungry after all that traipsing."

One step. Two steps. Three.

"Fine," she says.

That's not good enough so I keep walking. Her footfalls catch up to me.

"I'm sorry." Her teeth will turn to dust if she keeps grinding them that hard.

"What was that?"

"I said I'm sorry," she says, stopping in front of me. "I'm sorry for skipping out on you when all you were trying to do is protect me."

"And?"

Her nose scrunches. "And I accept your offer of security."

"Was that so hard?" I ask, handing over the bag of beignets.

CHAPTER FIVE

The first ballet school was established in 1661 by King Louis XVI, who danced in the ballets, sometimes in multiple roles in the same ballet.

BETHANY, FIVE YEARS EARLIER

I DODGE CARS and tour buses and horse-drawn carriages across the street.

The dance studio dots the edge of the French Quarter, which means it's packed with tourists day and night. Between those times, there's an uneasy quiet, a softer hum anticipating the night ahead.

Humid air boils the city. I'm wearing sweatpants and a loose T-shirt because they're easy to throw over my leotard and tights. I don't like lingering in the studio after class.

The shop below sells cigars and maybe other things. Illegal things.

A group of men always seems to gather on the street in front of it, smoking and swearing. More men as the night goes on. They give me looks as I go by, no matter what I'm wearing. Once, practice ran late. A man cornered me behind the cracked stone column.

He kept me there for hours, or maybe only seconds, before I kneed him between his legs. Curse words followed me into the cemetery as I dashed away.

Now I make it a point never to be outside when it's dark.

The cracked sidewalk pulls me along the outside of a cemetery. Sunlight peeks around statues and monuments, the structures that house the dead sometimes grander than the ones we live in. In the corner, wrought iron curls away from its crushed-stone corner. A hundred years of vagrants have worn away the rock. I pull my messenger bag close to my body so I can squeeze through. Damp fills my lungs, that familiar scent of rot and sickly sweet flowers. A trail of dirt guides me through the cemetery—the shortest distance through without stepping on graves.

I'm focused on the scrubby toes of my sneakers.

A shadow is my only warning. It moves. My heart rampages through my chest, and I look up suddenly, blinding myself. A large male body swings into view. Someone strong. Someone holding a white paper bag with the words *Café du Monde.*

"A peace offering," he says, holding it out.

I make myself breathe deep and slow. *Calm down, Bethany.* The scent of fried dough makes my mouth water. I can almost feel the powder dissolving on my tongue. "No, thanks."

He shrugs and tosses the bag onto the grass. "Suit yourself."

Before I can think it through, I snatch it up. "Don't do that."

A smirk. He must know how badly I want these beignets. Cafe du Monde makes the best in the world. "Thought you might be hungry. Your teacher's a real bitch, isn't she?"

I continue walking on the path, the heavy bag clutched in my fist, and he falls into step beside me. My teacher is a bitch, but I'm not about to agree with him. She's mean, but she's good. Every time she corrects my form, every time she shouts, *again,* every time she slaps a ruler against my thigh for missing the beat, I'm one step closer to leaving this city.

"Are you stalking me?" I ask, reaching into the bag. God, there must be ten of them in here. Still warm. I pinch off a large chunk and put it in my mouth. Yeast. Sugar. It tastes like pure heaven. I'm not sure it would be bad to have a stalker if he brought beignets.

"Your brother asked me to." He snorts. "A bit like the fox watching the henhouse."

I pause only a moment in bringing the beignet to my mouth. *Don't let him see you afraid. Don't let him see you weak.* "You're not a fox. I'm not a hen."

Those sharp green eyes don't miss a goddamn beat. He sees my hesitation. Maybe he even sees my fear. Knowledge can be a weapon, and this man seems especially dangerous. "More afraid of your brother than me, are you? What does the fucker do to you?"

"He doesn't touch me." Too much bravado. It sounds like a lie.

"Should I kill him for you?" The question comes out light, almost playful. It makes my heart skip a beat. These are the kind of men my brother makes friends with. Killers.

"No."

He glances sideways at a particularly intricate angel spreading her wings above a crypt. "You sure? I wouldn't mind. It would give me some-thing to do besides drink and fuck."

My stomach clenches around the bites I've

taken. I force the rest of the beignet into my mouth. I'm sure my lips are covered in white powder. "You're an asshole."

He grins, unrepentant. "Why do you think I get along with your brother?"

I pull out another beignet before shoving the rest into my messenger bag. They aren't exactly expensive, but there's never extra money for sweets. Not when there are rips in my leotards and holes in my shoes. "Don't let him hear you talk like that. Even if you're joking."

Then he's standing in front of me, moving so swift and quiet that I almost run into him. I'm around dancers every afternoon. Athletes. It still takes me by surprise. How does a soldier move with such grace? "Awww, are you worried for my safety? You think your brother is going to bury me in one of these unmarked plots?"

You wouldn't be the first one. I don't share that part. This man doesn't deserve my protection. He hasn't earned it, not even with the sugary goodness in my messenger bag. Dinner. That's what I'll eat for dinner. It will be a welcome respite from endless spicy stew. "He really asked you to follow me?"

"Wanted me to make sure you got home safe."

More likely he wanted to make sure I didn't take a detour. My brother has a lot of friends in this city. He has even more enemies. I wonder how much Josh knows about that. "Who would want to hurt me?" I ask, keeping my tone light.

We reach the end of the cemetery. There's no break in the iron here—only a low tomb that serves as a stepping stone. I hitch myself up and grab the arrows at the top of the fence. With a grunt I swing myself over. I land with an inelegant thud, the messenger bag slapping against my hip. Josh barely makes a sound when he follows me over. Most people don't realize it's easy to throw your body weight around. Muscles and inertia go a long way. It's much harder to control the fall, to pull your punch. It's much harder to be soft.

"Thanks for the beignets," I say, squinting into the sunlight. I can see my house from here, the yellow gate, the black roof. The shards of glass dotting the top of the concrete fence. "In return I'm going to give you some free advice. Go away. Go back where you came from or anywhere at all. New Orleans has nothing good to offer you."

It's not hard to see that my brother has plans for this man. He's skilled and without morals— the perfect employee for my brother's business. Plenty of people have come and gone. Most disappear without a word. I never know if they've left or ended up dead. For some reason it matters that Josh doesn't follow in their footsteps. The money isn't worth losing your soul.

Josh leans back against the iron gate, crossing his arms in a pose of supreme relaxation. I can almost pretend I don't see his alert emerald gaze or the bulk of a gun beneath his T-shirt. "You turn and turn and turn, like one of those ballet figures in a music box. Don't you ever want to break out of the mold? Do something other than a pretty little plié?"

Every time I breathe. "You don't know anything about my plans."

"I know you're afraid of something. And I know it's not me. Call me jaded, but that's pretty fucking interesting. I'm used to being the most scary motherfucker in the room."

A reluctant smile tugs at my lips. "Goodbye, Josh."

I already have my back to him when his reply floats on the heavy breeze. "You're wrong about one thing," he says, his voice rich in the humid air. "New Orleans has something good to offer me. It has you."

Probably a guy like this should be given the last word, but I've been flirting with danger too long to let him. There's something about Josh that calls me to tease him. I blow him a kiss with an exaggerated wave of my hand. *Goodbye, goodbye.*

CHAPTER SIX

*Bill Sikes, a vicious thug in the novel Oliver, was
probably named after a merchant who lived near
Dickens when he was a teenager.*

JOSH, FIVE YEARS EARLIER

I'VE BEEN ALL over the world, but one bar looks like another one. Sloppy drunk girls and opportunistic motherfuckers hoping to fuck. That used to be me. It *should* be me. Instead I'm nursing the same Jack and Coke since I got here while Caleb feels up the third chick in a row.

They're practically fucking at the table, her legs draped over his, his tongue in her mouth. I should take one of these girls into a grimy bathroom and fuck the tension out of my body. Instead I'm running my finger along condensation, cold where she'd be hot, imagining the sheen of sweat on a certain dancer's skin. That dancer will be tucked into bed now. Big brother keeps a tight watch on her, which is pretty fucking hypocritical considering how he treats the girls in the bar. Caleb gives the pretty blonde a shove, sending her staggering on high heels toward a packed table with her friends.

"We have business," he tells her. "Come back later." And she goes, flushed, clothes askew. The group swallows her into a tangle of limbs and drinks. She'll probably get fucked by someone else before Caleb takes her home. I'm not judging her. This is the life I live, too. It's rough and dirty, the grime so thick no Clorox could make it clean.

We've got a square table for the two of us, which is practically VIP treatment in a place like this. He turns to me, and his tongue darts out to wet his lip. I keep my grip loose on the thick glass cradled in my palm. Let him think I'm only here for his business. The boss wants my eyes open on this trip to the bar, as if my eyes are ever really closed. That's an excellent way to get a knife in the back...or the front. The characters in my part of the world are rarely much for subtlety. Caleb is no exception. He leans back in his seat, his dark eyes sweeping over the bar. "Ah—there they are."

Two men muscle their way through the crowd, headed straight for us. Noah and Connor are obvious choices, even for Caleb. Connor walks with a swagger. He turns heads all through the bar. Every move he makes is an invitation to look at him. He pulls in everyone's attention and lets it settle over his shoulders like the cheap yellow light of the bar is a goddamn spotlight. Connor loves the big entrance like he loves a good fuck. It almost makes up for the fact that he's got a weird scar like a part in his hair. A combat injury he loves to work for the women.

The man behind him wants no part of the attention. He wears a scowl that sucks the light from around Connor and brings the bar back to equilibrium. If Connor pulls everyone in, Noah pushes everyone away. Summer heat followed by a cold snap. I've heard whispers in dark corners about how things ended with one of his patrol partners after they got into a fight. Even with the gun at my side I still wouldn't relish a disagreement with Noah tonight.

Caleb stands to greet them with handshakes hard enough to crush bone, and the three of them squeeze back around the table. "Next time I call a meeting, be on time."

Connor raises his hands, a smile playing at the corners of his lips. "Got caught up. Didn't mean to halt the proceedings." He and Caleb exchange a look.

"No need to be coy," I tell them. "If you have

something to discuss, then say it." I don't know how much longer I can sit here with that dancer's body in a naked arabesque at the edges of my mind, wondering how smooth her skin would be under my rough palms, how warm and soft and clean.

A gleam flashes in Caleb's eyes. He leans forward in his chair, revealing how much he wants this—how much he needs men of my skill and lack of morals. "I brought you here to present an…opportunity."

The next sip of my Jack and Coke feels filthy against my tongue, like something might be swimming in it. Opportunity means black trucks parked outside warehouses. It means unloading thick cases in the dead of night. It means duffel bags stuffed with money and smelling like the desert.

It means weapons in the hands of men who look at us like meat waiting to be carved.

Noah leans against the wall, arms crossed.

I arch an eyebrow at Caleb. "Which is?"

"I'll reveal the details when you're ready to hear them. When I trust you more." He lifts a shoulder. "For now all you need to know is that it will be worth your time."

Which means the paycheck will be good. I

wish I could wipe the bitter taste off my tongue with one of those unmarked bills, but I know as well as anyone that it won't work.

I spin the glass around on the table, walking my fingers around the edge. Once upon a time I raised my right hand and swore to support and defend the constitution of the United States. Empty words for an empty soul. I did that for the paycheck, too. And a ticket out of hell. Now he's offering me even more money. I should jump at the chance—not so I can become a snitch, but so I can make something out of my life.

I'm not a fucking hero. Never have been. "How much?"

Caleb lets out a laugh sharper than a knife. "More than you'll know how to spend. As long as you come through for me. You get the job done. You don't ask questions."

Of course I wouldn't. Not if I'm the man Caleb believes me to be. And I'll be that man tonight. As for the other nights, I can't make any promises. The table nearby, men with bad intentions, the women and booze they'll use to accomplish them, seethes with laughter. A glass crashes to the floor. One more layer of spilled beer coats the wood.

"Listen." Caleb leans in. "We've got more

deals on the table, and we can't take them all on unless we have some help. From people who won't fuck us over."

If I were a better man, I'd stand up and tell him that eventually, their illegal arms trading absolutely will fuck him over. In fact, it probably already has, out there in mountain ranges across the ocean. But what would I gain by doing that? I'd be shutting out two chances to waste Caleb instead of one. And I'm not a better man.

Because while half of my mind is scanning Caleb's features for a sign that he's trying to screw with me, the other half is back in that shithole of a warehouse. The ghost of Bethany's lips on mine whispers over my skin. I'd fuck her just as soon as I'd kill him. I'd do one after the other. Of course, I'd prefer to fuck her with her brother safely underground.

"I have other business." I push my chair back and stand up, tossing a bill down on the table. Caleb tenses, his eyes following my every move. This business involves inappropriate thoughts about his sister and a locked bathroom door.

"So you're in, then."

I look Caleb in the eye. "I'll let you know."

Fuck this decision. I push back, ignoring the fact that Connor follows me out. They don't get an answer right away. Only he isn't coming to pressure me into agreeing.

Later I'll figure out whether I accept for myself or on behalf of the US government. Later I'll decide whether I become villain or hero. Right now there's only one place I want to be, and that's between the legs of a girl much too pure for me.

"You going after Bethany?"

I stop walking but don't turn around. How did he know? I must have given myself away more than I thought. Or maybe that's how Caleb keeps the dirty fuckers in line, by dangling that jailbait pussy in front of us. Maybe that's why he asked me to follow her home.

Don't punch Connor in the face. I glare him. "What's it to you?"

"She's a nice piece of ass. Not much in the way of tits, but—"

"Is there a point to this?"

"The point is you don't want to fuck with her. If there's one way to make sure Caleb puts a bullet in your back, it's to make a move toward his sister."

Interesting.

"Because I'm white?" It hasn't escaped my notice that even in the melting pot of New Orleans, couples of mixed race get some sideways glances. I wouldn't put it past Caleb to insist on that dynastic bullshit.

"Nah, he doesn't want anyone touching her. Or even looking at her. Including me. One time I talked about her ass, and he almost broke my jaw. You hear him talk, you'd think she was six years old instead of sixteen."

Caleb may be a crazy fuck, but I can't blame him for being protective of his sister. Sixteen years old? I don't usually mess around with jailbait. Then again, I'm not ready to walk away from her either. "Keep track of your own dick. Don't worry about mine."

CHAPTER SEVEN

*The contemporary circus Cirque du Soleil started as
a group of street performers who did acts like fire-
breathing and juggling on the streets of Quebec.*

BETHANY, FIVE YEARS EARLIER

LOW VOICES RUMBLE beneath the floor.

Mamere makes most of her money from
her regular weekly customers who want tarot card
readings. We're a few blocks away from the
French Quarter. Occasionally the tourists wander
far enough away to see the neon sign announcing
Palm Readings in the front window. I'm used to
doing my homework in the kitchen listening to
her croon her predictions through the velvet
curtains. It's comforting, her voice. Everything
comforts me except for the séances. They don't
happen very often. But they always, always, always
end in disaster. There's sobbing. Usually someone
throws something. Once the curtains caught on
fire. I'm trying to do my usual stretches before

bed, pretending like there isn't a grieving family clutching their hands beneath me. I'm already wearing my jammies—a pink tank top and purple shorts. I'm sitting with my right leg in front of me, my left behind in a side split. My science textbook is propped up by my foot, and I'm settled in to read this chapter before I switch sides.

Pop. I jump at the sound and scramble up from the floor. The textbook slams flat. Goosebumps rise on my arms. I don't believe in the séance happening underneath me, but the idea still freaks me out. *You didn't hear anything, Bethany. It was the wind.*

Pop. The sound comes again, and a squeak escapes me.

I creep up to the window, where I expect to see nothing in the backyard. Instead there's someone standing right underneath my window, looking up. My heart skips a beat. It's him.

Pebbles. It was Josh throwing pebbles at the window, not spirits blowing by on the wind. My cheeks heat, even though he can't have known what I was thinking.

I shove the window harder than I need to, with a bold push. The last thing I want is for him to think I was scared of a few pebbles. The night air wafts in, heavy with the scent of gumbo and hibiscus from the garden plants near the fence. "What are you doing here?" My heart thumps in a one-two-one-two beat at the sight of his face tilted up toward mine. The memory of powdered sugar ghosts across my tongue. It's almost impossible to associate his hard body with soft, warm beignets. He is not soft, I remind myself. He is the same man who stalked around me in the warehouse and made my pulse race. If he's really working with Caleb, he's far more dangerous than the average man lurking in the city's cemeteries. *Far* more dangerous.

"Come down," he tells me. The tone of his voice is light. Simple—just go down. I should shut the window and lock it. But a flimsy window lock would never keep Josh out. I'm not even sure I'd want it to. Voices rise beneath the floor. Mamere's made contact, it sounds like. This is the perfect time to leave. I'd almost risk walking right out, but then I'd have to pass by her. If it interrupts the séance it'll inspire another lecture. Mamere is afraid I'll become like my mother. A stripper by the time she was my age. Pregnant with Caleb by nineteen. It wasn't the path Mamere wanted for my mother, and it's not the one I'm taking. That doesn't stop Mamere from wringing her hands about it.

So I slip on my shoes and go out the window instead.

The old windowsills are wide and sturdy, and my dancer's body has no problem finding footholds on the way down. The difference now is that Josh is watching. He doesn't step forward to offer a hand. He lets me choose my own descent. My last stop is a strand of ivy that stretches across the house. I predict it'll hold my weight for the breath I need to get a toehold on the frame on the window below. I'm right. Gravity and I shake hands and I land lightly on my feet, letting my knees absorb some of the shock from the grass.

Now Josh and I are restored to our natural order.

He grins down at me. "Love the outfit."

My face flushes all the way down to my chest. I didn't dress for company, clearly. "You asked me to come down. I'm assuming I don't need formal wear for that."

Not that I have a lot of formal wear. I have one thrifted gown I got for the homecoming dance last year. One size up, so I could wear it again this year with different accessories.

And not that Josh asked me to come down. He didn't.

He *told* me to, and I obeyed him.

"So," he says. "Psychic Readings for twenty bucks."

I roll my eyes. "That's my grandmother."

"You don't believe she's psychic."

"It's just a bunch of smoke and mirrors." Sometimes she does feel psychic. Even my brother has an uncanny sense about people. I'm lucky my brother's not inside. He'd have sensed this by now. No part of me wants to find out what would happen if he saw me standing with Josh at an unscheduled time like this.

Maybe a small part.

No—that would be awful.

My shoulder lifts. "When people come in through the front parlor there's incense and curtains. Even a few voodoo dolls to complete the effect. I've seen the place in the early morning, with a cup of coffee by the crystal ball and my math textbook under the tarot deck."

"It's like sausage."

"Pardon?"

"You've seen how the sausage gets made. Now you don't want to eat it."

That makes me snort. "Are you disappointed? Maybe you wanted me to tell you your fortune. Maybe that's why you came."

"Maybe," he says. "Maybe not. The future's a

71

scary place."

My eyebrows raise. We have enough people coming to the house desperate for answers. It's strange to meet someone who doesn't seem to want them.

He tilts his head toward the back of the yard. "Let's go."

My pulse is a drumbeat that won't settle. You'd think I'd just run through our entire recital routine from the way my heart pounds. "Where?"

"For a walk. Where else?"

Where else indeed. Now I wish I'd put something else on. Not because it's cold, but because the tank top is flimsy. The bralette I'm wearing underneath isn't meant to conceal anything from the world. It's meant for someone who will spend the night tucked under the covers. We cross the yard, staying close to the deepest shadows. I can only relax once we're past the ring of light from the house—and I can't relax much.

Of all the shifting shadows by the creek bed, Josh is by far the biggest. And scariest. But I'm not about to show him that.

Wind whispers through the Spanish moss dangling from the branches of the live oak tree. It's humid, the way it always is in New Orleans. The moisture in the air gives it a tactile quality. It reminds me of the way Josh kissed me in the warehouse before he knew who I was. Before I knew who he was.

"I saw your brother tonight." His voice is low, a sultry match for the night breeze against the corner of my mouth. It's like he sensed the spirit between us—my brother, my savior and my enemy. A brick wall between me and Josh.

A chill battles with the heat at the base of my spine. "Yeah? I'm sure a lot of people saw him tonight. He wasn't home."

"Do you know where he was?"

This feels like a test. Most of the tests in my life have simple answers, like *igneous rock* or *it's an arabesque, not a pirouette, do it again.* The truth in tonight's case is equally as simple. Only I'm not sure if it's the right answer. "No. He doesn't tell me his plans before he goes out. I don't know anybody who has an older brother like that."

"My older brother let me know where he was going," Josh muses. "It didn't make much of a difference once he left for the army, though." His tone bristles with something underneath I don't dare ask about. I can only feel it, like the thrum of voices beneath the floor in my house.

We meander down closer to the creek, where the dry bed narrows. Josh steps closer, and his arm brushes against mine. "How much do you know about the company your brother keeps?" He stops suddenly, facing me in the moonlight. *Mistake*, screams the voice in the back of my mind. *You shouldn't have come here.* But damn it, I wanted to.

"He meets with dangerous men. He *is* dangerous. I've told you that before. You don't need me to tell you again." I'm outside, out of sight, with the most dangerous man of all. But it's not pure terror that makes goosebumps prick my skin. It's something more akin to excitement. Adrenaline. "What's this about?"

Josh waits a beat, then turns and keeps walking. He doesn't speak until I've caught up with him. "He called an interesting meeting tonight. A man named Noah joined us at the bar."

I should turn around right now and run for the house. I should stay far, *far* away from Josh. I should, at the very least, rectify this grave error I've made. But I do none of those things. "Yeah? What was he like?"

"He was quiet."

Of all the words Josh could have chosen, this one has to be the most...unexpected. "Quiet?"

"Silent." Josh shakes his head. "It was fucking eerie, is what it was. It made me wonder if the rumors are true. I've heard one in particular that stands out."

I can't help myself. "What was it?"

He does a slow turn, and it's with a mixture of relief and disappointment that I realize he's walking me back to my house. "I heard he had a disagreement with one of his patrol partners, once upon a time. That man went on rounds one night and ended up with a bullet in his brain." He says it so lightly, like he might be telling me about the high school yearbook or a football score. Fear wraps around my belly and pulls tight. We cross back over the boundary into the backyard. Josh leans in close. So close that his breath tickles the shell of my ear. His lips brush the delicate skin there. "The official record says the man was killed in action."

I suck in a breath. "Are you afraid of him?"

"I probably should be. There are worse things in the night. *Auribus teneo lupum.* Have you heard that before?"

"Latin?"

"Yep. It means you're fucked either way. That's what I am in this situation, between your brother and Noah and the US Army—and you. You, most of all."

"What are you talking about?"

"Goodnight, Bethany." He turns to go as abruptly as he appeared.

The swing creaks in the night breeze against a backdrop of crickets. A fresh wave of goosebumps and heat erupts over my skin. "You came here to tell me that?"

"No," he says over his shoulder, his figure already disappearing into the night. "I came here to see your face."

BETHANY, PRESENT TIME

AT THE END of the day I walk down the concrete steps. A man in a black T-shirt and tactical pants leans against a black SUV, his face framed by sunlight. Even before I get close, I know it isn't Josh. Disappointment weighs heavy in my stomach. I shouldn't care about Joshua North. In fact I should be relieved that he's sent someone else. Features form out of the shadows. Noah. Panic seizes my body for a heartbeat. Only when my foot touches the next step can I breathe again. I'm not a dumb teenager anymore. I'm not at the mercy of violent men anymore. That includes Josh.

"Fancy meeting you here," I say.

A curt nod. "Ma'am."

That makes me snort. "What are you doing here?"

He opens the back door for me. "Escorting you home."

"Where exactly is home?"

"A safe location."

"I knew you didn't mean my apartment. That would be too easy. Has it occurred to you that Josh is doing exactly what my brother did? Having me watched? Controlling where I go?"

"Do you need to stop somewhere on the way?" he asks, his tone bland.

I glare at the open door with its cool leather seats. Does it have to look so appealing? I want the safety the dark interior promises. That's always been the problem with Josh. I want what he offers, but I know better than to trust it. "Does North Security keep safe houses in every city? That seems excessive."

A pause. He doesn't stop scanning the perimeter even as he answers, "This isn't a North Security property."

"Then who owns it?"

Those dark eyes meet mine, bringing with them a flash of painful memory. When I was young and foolish and halfway in love. "Joshua North."

Josh owns property in New Orleans? Why the hell would he want to? He was only ever here for Caleb. Maybe that's still why he's here. To keep tabs on the man he once brought down. It couldn't possibly be for the little sister who gave her heart away. There's no way this ends well. No way this leaves me anything but heartbroken all over again.

The allure is too strong. Even safety I might have been able to withstand. It's the curiosity that propels me inside the back of the SUV. That I'll be able to see a place that Josh calls his own.

I settle into the leather seats, holding back a groan as the plush cushion meets my aching muscles. It's not like I enjoy using public transportation, clutching a frayed leather strap for the stop-start ride. I don't enjoy being bumped or groped. I don't enjoy shielding my wallet deep in my purse so I'll still have it, but I do enjoy the independence that comes with it. I can afford the bus, and that makes it the only choice for me. I never want to ask my brother for help.

The life of a dancer isn't a lucrative one. The New York Times praised my dancing as "a revelation." A two-inch write-up in Vogue called me "incandescent." Unfortunately most landlords don't accept critical praise as currency to pay rent.

The position with the avant-garde dance company is enough for me. Unless I'm being stalked by some crazy fan. That's been hard to accept. Sometimes people talk to me like I should have limos and private security—who's going to pay for that?

Joshua North, apparently.

I seriously doubt Landon is paying North Security a single cent.

The idea makes me uncomfortable. I don't like owing anyone anything. Because you never know when they'll call in the favors. You never know what they'll be. I learned that lesson young.

What will Joshua expect me to owe him? Nothing good.

The black SUV slows down in an alley lined with large bungalows. Heavy hydrangeas lean over a tall concrete wall. A pink building stands behind it, its black iron balcony quintessentially New Orleans. A row of black windows reflects the city without giving a glimpse of what's inside. I study the different apartments, wondering which one would give the best tactical advantage. Wondering what it would be like to live life as Joshua North, always aware of the threats around him. "Which one is his?"

Dark eyes in the rearview mirror. "The whole

building."

The whole building. Jesus. Something like this probably costs millions of dollars. Since when did he get that rich? Not through selling illegal weapons from the US Army. I suppose there's plenty of money being the good guy, too. Being the hero. He'd hate to be called that, but it's the truth.

I step into the building with a nervous flutter in my stomach. There are a million reasons why Josh and I will never be together. I knew them already. Now there's one more—the absolute grandeur of this old-fashioned mansion, one of the few that hasn't been chopped into tiny apartments. We belong to different worlds. His is sharp enough to cut me. Mine is already in pieces.

CHAPTER EIGHT

The musical Oliver!, based on Dickens's novel, has been performed in more than 20 languages, including Basque, Faroese, and Icelandic. Musicians who have played the part of the Artful Dodger include Phil Collins and Davy Jones of the Monkees.

JOSH, PRESENT TIME

B ETHANY APPEARS AT my door as a shadow. That's all it takes to make my cock wake the fuck up, that hint of her against the frosted security glass of my front door. The porch light makes her shadow look carved, all hard edges. But when I open the door, she's transformed back into herself. There is a certain toughness about her that reminds me in a vague way of her brother.

She lifts her chin. A challenge. I thought I saw a flash of vulnerability there, as if maybe she's worried about her welcome, but I must have imagined it.

And yet…she's standing on my doorstep.

I scan behind the both of them for any sign someone else has breached the gate. There are none. Noah's face stands out against the black SUV, the curt nod visible even from here.

Bethany takes a single step across the threshold. The scent of lotion reaches out and lodges deep in my lungs. It pulls hard enough to tear. I ignore it. Shut the door behind her. Flip the lock. The deadbolt, in comparison to the rest of my personal security system, is just for show. Like the way I'm giving her a stoic expression. The real walls, they're deep where no one can see. Where she'll never breach them.

What is the purpose of denial?

Survival. That's the purpose.

Bethany watches me, dark eyes alive in the low, warm light of my entryway. "You sent Noah to pick me up instead of coming yourself?"

"I took a calculated risk." I calculate another form of risk and take a step back to put some space between us. Nobody, least of all Bethany, needs to know how much I want to take two steps forward. Surround her. Consume her. *No—not that.*

That raw scrape burrows into my gut. Hunger.

She's got a hand on her hip. She's pissed,

which I shouldn't find so hot. "A pretty bold move, thinking I'd go along with this if it was Noah and not you."

The smirk that flashes across my face is mostly a cover for the way her voice makes me feel. "It worked, didn't it? You're here."

"For now." It seems to take her some effort to tear her eyes away from mine. She examines the gleaming scarred wood and polished brass with a look of apprehension, as if I'd decorated the place with guns and bombs instead. Those beautiful brown eyes meet mine again. They're darker this time. Bethany drops her shoulders a fraction of an inch. "Where do you expect me to sleep? If I stay here?"

I'm seized by the powerful urge to take her hand in mine and trace the line of her palm. *See? That lifeline is already longer, you pretty little fool. I'm keeping you alive.* Instead I gesture toward the grand staircase. "Upstairs."

She follows me up each step, footfalls so soft I can barely hear them. My vision sharpens as we reach the top landing. I try not to make the baseline assumption that my home is safe. That's the kind of complacency that will get you killed. But there's nothing in the hall to suggest that anything is out of the ordinary.

Only Bethany.

I lead her toward the back of the house and into the master suite. The sitting area is quiet, peaceful. A fire burns in the grate. I have it low enough so the temperature remains comfortable. A set of wide double doors stands open, revealing a bed with white sheets and a fluffy white bedspread.

"This is nice," Bethany says on an exhale that almost, *almost*, becomes a sigh.

"Nicer than that shithole you came from. And there's no need to keep the windows open. They sprang for central air conditioning and every-thing."

Her glance is a slice. A little cut. "You seem personally offended by my apartment."

"I'm personally offended by your total disre-gard for your own safety. Especially while you're getting threats. Coming here is the first good decision you've made."

She lets out a short laugh. "I wouldn't call it a good decision."

"Better than staying there, where anyone can reach you. When did you start getting the letters? Why didn't you at least call Liam when you got it?"

Bethany blinks at the abrupt change in topic,

but I need to focus on something other than the way she looks in her heather-gray hoodie and leggings. Best to focus on the job at hand. Which is not, unfortunately, stripping that hoodie off to reveal soft, brown skin. "The letters are personal," she says flatly. "I told you that."

"And I told you that was bullshit."

A slight narrowing of her eyes. "They *are* personal." The fire in her eyes burns low in my belly. "And you're overreacting anyway. They're nothing."

"I'm not sure you're the best judge of that."

Bethany's eyes flick away, her breasts rising underneath the hoodie. Her grip tightens on the bag slung over her shoulder. It's ripped. Frayed. Ancient. "And what makes you a better judge? The fact that you got a job at North Security?"

"The fact that I'm head of operations at North Security, more like. I'm not some grunt who needs to kiss the boss's ass."

The hint of a smile chases across her lips and disappears. "Don't pretend that protecting me is going to impress anybody else."

"It should, since you're making it a damn nightmare."

"Have you seen the stuff Samantha gets?" she demands, referring to the world-class violinist my brother's with. "You stand on a stage, people are going to have an opinion about that. If I was worried about what some nutjob thinks, I could never put on my ballet shoes. Is that what you want?"

There's a pang in my chest. It's where a heart would be, if I had one. We go to battle every day, but we have guns and knives and armor. She has cardboard soles and silk ribbons. She goes to battle every day armed with absolutely nothing.

Bethany stretches her arms over her head. This has the effect of making the hoodie rise until I can see a line of brown flesh. My palms ache to touch it. To run my fingertips over it. To push up the shirt underneath the hoodie until every last bit of her is open to the air. Open to me. But I don't. Instead, I watch her fake a yawn.

Message received. "Sleep if you want."

She drops her arms to her sides, eyes searching mine. "You don't go to bed this early."

"If you think I'm going to bed, sweetheart, you're sorely mistaken."

"Where are you going to be, then?" Her voice is shaky, as if I might crawl into bed with her. Maybe demand payment for my protection with her pretty little body.

I gesture to the sofa. "Right here."

"All night?"

"All night." There are extra bedrooms upstairs. Sometimes Liam and Samantha use them when they visit. It's more comfortable here than the official North Security safe house. There's no way I'd be on a different floor from Bethany. I'm not even going to be more than fifteen feet from her. I'm right outside the door, in this parlor outside the bedroom, like an overmuscled guard dog keeping intruders away.

She gives me a long look. I expect more arguments, so it's a surprise when she turns to flit into the bedroom, light on her feet. My heart thrashes against my rib cage. It wants to follow her. The last blaze of the sunset burns itself out against the windowpanes, and I sit on the sofa.

Every sound hangs against the backdrop of her, in my space. Running the water in the bathroom. On, off, on, and then off again. Is she naked? I'm imagining the strong, subtle curves of her body, sleek muscle beneath dark skin, the dusky color of her nipples and her pussy. Why can't I stop fucking thinking about it? The soft click of the doors shutting behind me.

A subtle creak when she climbs into bed.

My sheets are going to smell like her. I may never wash them again, even when she leaves.

Because if there's one thing that's certain in all this, it's that she'll leave. Once the letters are taken care of, once I've pissed her off enough.

I listen to my own heart slowing into a steady rhythm. To the house settling on its foundation. The high call of a Mississippi kite soaring overhead outside. The air is heavy with her presence. It makes no sense. She's too light to weigh on me this much. She probably weighs a hundred and fifteen pounds soaking wet. But every breath she takes shifts the air in the house. It's like the tide.

Only twenty minutes have passed when I hear the whisper of her feet on the carpet. The moon hangs in the great oak tree. Shadows cover me like a goddamn blanket.

Bethany's voice is tentative, as if she's afraid to wake me. "Josh?"

I shift my body on the sofa. "Yeah?"

"I can't fall asleep." She says this in the same tone that she used to announce that she had to pee last night at her apartment. The matter-of-factness makes my heart ache. "I thought I'd sit out here. If...that's okay."

"I never took you for the type to ask permission." Christ. I could have said *of course, that's fine. Come sit here. I'll go. I'll stay. Whatever you need.* But instead I throw my arm over the back of the sofa. "Not like I was sleeping, either."

The sofa bows underneath her when she sits, tucking one leg up and letting the other one dangle. Her toes brush against the carpet. The flames in the fireplace, steady and strong, are echoed in her eyes. Silence draws itself over us like a throw blanket. Bethany lets it come down. After a minute she shrugs it off with a deep breath. "I didn't picture you living in a house like this. I thought it would be…" She searches for the next word on the ceiling. "Less nice."

I huff a laugh. "To match my dead, withered soul? You know better than that." Her brother loved the finer things in life, too. In the end that's what made him vulnerable. He wanted more than men like us could ever have.

"I do," she admits softly, not looking at me.

The question fights its way past my lips in spite of every instinct screaming that to ask it is to admit to some…connection…with Bethany. Some intimacy. A past. "Why? Why did you ask me to spare him, knowing what he did?"

Her expression looks stricken. She turns to her lap for answers. "I didn't think we were going to talk about that. Not ever again, honestly."

"It would be easier that way," I admit, turning

toward her, closing the space between us on the sofa. Every breath is laced with her scent. "Sometimes I don't pick the easy route. Sometimes I'm fucking allergic to it."

The flinch tells me I've hit a nerve. "Yeah," she says on a sudden gust of breath. "Yeah, me too. It's almost scary when things are too peaceful."

My heart ricochets across my chest. "I know the feeling."

The silence stretches out and then compresses, thickening by the second. When Bethany speaks, it's a terrible relief. "When I was six years old, my dad came home. Drunk." The fire flickers in her brown eyes. "He came after me. He started raving about how I was just like my mom, and how I'd turn out like her, how he'd kill me before he let me do that. I was so scared and…I thought that was it. I thought I would die that night."

I dig my nails into my palms. *Motherfucker.*

Bethany clears her throat. "Caleb was only twelve and he wasn't—he wasn't like he is now. Not that strong. Not that ruthless. But he stood up to our dad. He protected me. In the process…" Her voice has taken on a wooden tone. "In the process my dad fell and hit his head."

"What happened?" I ask the question to break

the new silence before it digs in and swallows us both. And I ask it because I have the sense I know what's coming.

Why Bethany still loved her brother. Why she asked me to do the impossible.

And why, for some reason, I actually did it.

My skin hums with the electricity of anticipation. Memories, one after the other. Her face, desperate and flushed. The way she said, *please*. And the way I said, *I wanted to fuck you. That's it*. Tears she wouldn't let fall in the corners of her eyes.

"It happened so fast. One minute he was hollering, and the next minute he was lying there, bleeding into the grass, not moving."

Fuck. "He died."

"You don't understand how scared we were, that Caleb would get sent away or locked up. We didn't know if they'd understand that he didn't mean to kill him—or if they'd even care. No one we knew trusted the cops."

She's wrong about one thing. I do understand the fear. That's something we have in common— an abusive father. No matter how much his fists hurt, I was more scared of the system, of the paperwork and the pity, of the wild unknown. My father was pain—and we understood pain very well.

"What did you do?"

"We covered it up. It took both of us to drag his body to the bayou behind our house. Pushed him in and left his fishing rod tangled in the weeds. Got our stories straight so when they principal came and took us out of class, we'd act surprised."

"No wonder you weren't spooked by a few letters. You grew up with a monster."

"We fought him together. We killed him together. We covered it up together. You can't do that with a person without tying a piece of your soul to them." She twines her fingers through each other and drops her hands into her lap. "I owed him my life. I still do."

"You don't owe him shit."

"That's why I asked you to spare him. Not because he deserved it. I know he doesn't. There's nothing that can excuse what he's done, but—"

"But what?"

"I keep thinking—what if that was the night that changed him? He could have grown up, gotten a law degree, become a CEO or something. Instead he became… a traitor. What if that night set him on that path?"

"Do you know how insane that sounds? You

aren't responsible for his decision to steal weapons and sell them to the highest bidder."

"Don't you ever feel guilt? Or is that too human for Joshua North? You just go around doing what you want and saying what you want with no consequences."

That's how it should be. That's how I pretend to be, but the truth is I feel guilt all the damn time. Guilt for leaving my younger brother. Guilt for wanting my older one to stay. We didn't kill our father, but we had our own nights of hell. Nights he pushed us into the well. He didn't throw down a rope until morning. I remember how my arms felt like jelly, but I held little Elijah out of the fetid water as long as I could. I remember how Liam sobbed from the ground, begging my father to let us out. *You can't do that with a person without tying a piece of your soul to them.*

Bethany and I had our own night of violence. I came to her covered in blood. She put herself into my debt with that favor. You can't do that with a person and walk away unscathed. A piece of her soul is tied to a piece of mine.

CHAPTER NINE

The first record of dancing appears in an Egyptian tomb dated about 3300 B.C. Dance has served many purposes throughout history, including entertainment, exercise, courtship, and worship in religious ceremonies.

BETHANY, PRESENT TIME

SOMETHING DARK FLASHES in Josh's eyes at the mention of me owing my brother anything. Like he knows what that means. He probably does, which would explain the black lightning across his emerald eyes. It feels like he's slammed down a gate in the air between us. Subtle shifts of his body turn him away from me. "You should get your beauty sleep."

My eyes burn, but I'm not sure if it's from fatigue or the whiplash of this conversation. I've never once expected Joshua North to be anything less than an arrogant asshole, cocky to the end. But I thought I felt him leaning into me as we spoke. Like the barbs in our words held no actual bite.

He jerks his head over his shoulder, so handsome it cuts me to the quick. "I mean it. Rest up for tomorrow."

My heart beats lightly, a hummingbird trapped in a cage. "Tomorrow will be like every other day."

His smirk wounds as much from its hard beauty as anything else. "Tomorrow, everything changes. You're with me now. And if you think I'm going to let you dangle yourself in front of all the fuckfaces of the world like a pretty prize, you're kidding yourself." With these last words he stands, his muscled frame silhouetted against the fire. He wears a white T-shirt over slacks I know are designed to conceal weapons. The pants skim the line of his hips in a sensual touch. I want to leap up and hook my hands under his elbow, using the graceful swing of my weight to pull him back down next to me. But of course I won't do that.

And maybe it's only the power of suggestion, but a certain tiredness comes over my muscles now. A heaviness. I leave him standing in the sitting area and pad back to the massive bed alone. I take a deep breath, like I'm waiting in the wings for the first strains of music to pull my arms and legs, like I'm held up by string. That's how it feels when I climb into bed, as if someone else does the heavy lifting.

Joshua North's sheets have to have a thread count in the thousands. They feel like silk against my skin compared to the secondhand set I got for the ratty twin mattress in my apartment. The pillowcase is very nearly silky enough to assuage my regrets about not bringing my own pillowcase, which was the one semi-expensive item of all my bedding, and absolutely necessary. I don't have the faintest clue what the protocol is in this situation. Do I leave him a note on the bedside table? *If you're going to keep me prisoner, I need a pillowcase that won't fuck with my hair.*

The bigger problem, of course, is that his bed smells like him. Like electricity and man and a stiff breeze.

As much as it pains me to admit it, he's right—I should get some sleep. But the moment my head hits the pillow, the reel of my memories begins. All of them suffused with his scent. With the ragged beating of my heart. I squeeze my eyes shut and try to guide my thoughts away from that night. I've tried so hard to forget it over the years, but the memory refuses to be anything less than crystal clear. That's what I get for talking about my father again.

He was so angry. That's the one part I can't get straight in my mind. What was he angry about? In the end it didn't matter, but the scared little girl in me can't stop wondering what I did wrong. I only knew that the way his face twisted and reddened meant something very, very bad. One foot stomped the floor, his hand slapped the kitchen counter, a macabre dance.

Give in and it'll be over quicker. It's what I thought then, and here I am, doing the same thing all this time later. Squeezing my eyes shut. Hoping for it to be over. Tasting the bitter acid at the back of my throat.

Back then I didn't see where Caleb came from. I heard him—I heard everything. The strangled sound he made as he threw himself between my father and me. My eyes snapped open in time to see him bury his fists in my father's shirt. My father's weight should have been too much for my brother, but he was drunk. Wasted. And he teetered. He leaned far to the right, swiping at Caleb. The set of my brother's shoulders looked like a man's, but he was young, his shoulder blades fine like a bird's wings.

How did it happen? It happened like this—

Caleb let go of our father's shirt. And because of the alcohol raging in our father's veins, he didn't fall backward, or sit down hard. His feet tangled underneath him, and he fell to the side. So many moments in our lives are decided by mere inches. A finger length can mean the difference between a solid landing and a broken ankle. Or a broken skull.

The crack of his head against the brick has me reaching for the blankets. So many years later, and I can still hear it as clearly as if it's happening here in the room. I pull the sheets tight without thinking. I'm covered in the scent of Josh's skin.

Caleb's face, stricken in the dingy yellow light of the kitchen. His mouth in a horrified grimace. The darkness pooling beneath my father's body.

But this time—this time—the sheets pull me back out of the narrative and into a strange, pulsing desire.

Because there are other memories. Memories I can't chase away, not when I'm lying in his bed. The last thing I want is Joshua North. He's too much like my brother—I know that. I *know* that. But the smell of him against my skin has heat curling through my belly. My skin tingles with the closeness of him. All that separates us is a few feet of empty air and an unlocked door. Once, he kissed the corner of my lips in a warehouse owned by my brother. His green eyes took in the lines of my body beneath my leotard, even then. Once, he bent to whisper a secret in my ear that made me feel like a grown-up instead of a child with my nose pressed to the window of a world I never wanted to be part of.

Once, I saw him sleeping—defenseless.

I traced the lines of his forehead and chased the dark thoughts away. He's not sleeping now; I can feel it. Just like I can feel his skin under my fingertips still. And his mouth against mine. God, it could have gone so much further. Back then, I questioned it. I ran through scenarios in my mind. What would I do if Joshua North lowered me to the ground outside and peeled off my shorts? What would I do if my panties were next? I know the answers now. I would have let him.

At some point my mind slips from a white-knuckled awareness into a half-sleep. Is that his heart I hear, beating in my ears, or is it my own? And why does it feel like it's somehow beating outside my chest, alongside the man who still sits on the sofa, guarding the door inside his own house?

The very last edges of my consciousness hear them—the raindrops. The night breeze tosses them gently against the windowpane by the bed. They can't touch me. Only the sound can reach me here. *Tap, tap, tap.*

CHAPTER TEN

In 2008, the world's first sustainable dance floor opened at Club Watt in Rotterdam, Sweden. The floor's tiles rest on springs wired to generators. The harder people dance, the more the springs are compressed and this converts into energy, which runs the LED lights in the floor.

JOSH, PRESENT TIME

MARLENA OPENS THE door to her townhouse with a flourish, her gauzy red sleeves accentuating the movement. Then the act cracks and she giggles, throwing her arms around Bethany's neck. "You're here! I'm so excited. And you brought your bodyguard." She shoots me a questioning look. "You know she's perfectly safe with me and Scott, right?"

"Now you'll all be perfectly safe." I give her a wide grin, like this is a fucking joke. It's the furthest thing from a joke. Having Bethany in my house is an exquisite torture. I thought agreeing to this little double date with Marlena and Scott Castle would help ease the tension. Surprise, surprise. It hasn't. Not yet. That's probably because Bethany would have climbed down the ivy on the side of my house if I didn't agree.

Marlena squeezes Bethany a little tighter—tight enough that I consider peeling her arms away from Bethany's skin one by one—and then releases her. "You look gorgeous," she tells her friend. "Everyone at the club is going to have their eyes on you. And I know there are so many guys in the city who'll make it worth your while." She winks at Bethany. My stomach lurches at the thought of Bethany in one of their lurid little deals.

What would you even call it? A sugar daddy? Prostitution. Marlena holds power in the city. If she'd been born a few decades earlier, she'd have been posted up at the Moulin Rouge. Or salons full of artists and courtesans in France. Instead she's bought and paid for at this brownstone, with its outrageously built-out doorframe and spiky wrought-iron fence rising out of brickwork at the front.

"Oh, stop." Bethany's voice is light, revealing nothing.

Does she want a sugar daddy? She might need

one. I've seen what that sad excuse for a dance company reports on its taxes. I'll pay her a million fucking dollars not sleep with one, even if she never touches me.

"I need tequila," Marlena announces. "Are we ready?"

As if she's summoned him, Scott Castle appears behind her. For a man in his fifties, he's pretty fit. His suit's probably bespoke from Italy or some shit like that. Not a single silver-blond strand of hair moves out of place. He slips a possessive hand on the curve of Marlena's waist. Like I'm going to try and duel him for her.

"I see our guests have arrived." He tugs her closer as he says it, brushing a kiss to the spill of her auburn hair. She's set it free for the evening. Bethany's remains in a tight, sculpted bun, not a wisp of hair out of place. Scott gives all of us a sharp-edged smile, then extends his hand to shake. "Joshua North. Your reputation precedes you. North Security has developed quite a reputation for quality work. I'm surprised you're working such a small detail personally."

His glance at Bethany tells me he's fishing for details. I'm not giving him a damn thing. "That's right. We have." I shake his hand once, hard, and let go.

"Will you be stepping in for drinks, or should we get going?" Scott raises his eyebrows. So fucking genteel. Bethany stands in graceful stillness next to me. People take stillness for granted. They think dance is all about movement. That life is all about movement. Bethany proves otherwise. The scent of her skin taunts me. Her stillness is a call to action. There were nights I could have gone into Marlena's home and sat on the creamy leather of her sofa and let her bring other women to me. That I might have swallowed too much of Scott's liquor and fucked myself into a blessed numbness.

Not tonight.

Tonight the four of us get into the Bentley that Scott keeps for Marlena and go to the French Quarter. Marlena's favorite club is a sleek three-story bar with views of the city on all sides and a valet staff that won't fuck up your car.

She makes us split a bottle of champagne on the way.

For some reason, with Bethany looking at me from beneath heavy lidded eyes, knowing other men are about to look at her body in that shimmery purple dress, I throw back a flute. By the time the driver pulls up in front of the velvet ropes demarcating the walk underneath the famous brick archway, the bubbles have infiltrated my blood.

It feels strangely like hope. And hope is always reckless.

Hope is always a mistake.

Marlena has her arm hooked through Bethany's as we take the staircase up to the second level. This place isn't crammed into a grimy basement that suffers from a permanent moisture problem. The shutters on the tall windows are thrown open wide. Music escapes them into the night, while humid air slips inside.

The club lights shine in Bethany's hair. That damn bun has been the bane of my existence since she walked into my house. It makes me ache to fit my palm underneath that bun and feel her body bend beneath my grip. Jesus. Five seconds in this club and I'm already harder than steel. I grit my teeth and tell my dick to calm the fuck down. Nothing's happening with me and Bethany. Not tonight. Not ever.

We split up long enough for Scott and me to get a round of drinks and for me to scan the place while the bartender works. More champagne for Marlena, who likes fun in every form. Jack and Coke for me. That will be the only drink I'll have tonight. Scott orders two fingers of thirty-year

Glenfiddich, downs it in one gulp, and slams the glass back onto the bar. His eyes narrow. "Where are they?"

I motion with my drink. Even from ten feet away, I've been aware of every move Bethany has made. I've been aware of every man in the room, every potential threat to her safety. "Over there. Dancing."

"Are you going to come? Or are you going to find a table?"

The old me would have planted myself at a table and let the women come to me. They always do. I'd have had one in my lap in five minutes flat. And you wouldn't have caught me dancing. But Marlena and Bethany circle each other, the bends of their bodies like water. Bethany's purple dress somehow manages to look regal. Every move she makes sings of power brewing under her skin. Her eyes catch mine. The hint of a smile. She knows I'm watching.

I throw back the Jack and Coke. The burn reminds me of the club I took her to that night five years ago. That one smelled like mildew and electricity. This one has the subtle scent of hydrangeas pumped in through the ventilation system. And just like then, I'll be damned if anybody else gets close.

BETHANY, PRESENT TIME

MARLENA PULLS ME into the bathroom at top speed, still laughing. "Oh my God." She twirls on tiptoe over to the sink, then grabs the porcelain with a wince. "Remind me not to do that again. My calf is killing me." Dying or not, her face is still flushed pink from the series of tequila shots she did after the champagne. "I'll probably have to ice it once Scott's done with me."

I lean into the mirror and pretend to examine my mascara. Done with her.

She says it so casually. It doesn't bother Marlena at all, trading her body for security in the present. She bangs her way into one of the stalls and lets out a satisfied sigh. "So Josh North is obsessed with you. That much is obvious."

"He's not," I say with a snort. "He's obsessed with getting a rise out of me. Always has been. He's an asshole."

"Awww, he is not. Deep down he's probably sweet."

My reflection is the only witness to my disbelief. "Marlena, he's not sweet. The North brothers aren't known for being sweet. Ever."

"Are you sure? I heard Liam's head over heels."

I swipe my finger and thumb over my eyebrows. "That's different. Getting married isn't the same thing as turning into a nice man. Neither is falling in love. And Josh is doing neither of those things. He's just an asshole."

"An asshole who brought you to the club and has been dancing with you all night. He's not bad, either." The toilet flushes, and Marlena waltzes back to the sink next to me. I perch on a stretch of marble countertop while she washes up. "He seems worried about you."

This time I swallow the snort that threatens to escape me. "Are we seeing the same guy? Because he doesn't seem worried to me. He seems…." Controlling. Insistent. He fills the room with his arrogance, and those glittering green eyes that see right through my carefully crafted facade. Like he knows. I'm playing the part of a cool and confident sitting duck. The breath goes out of me at the thought. I work hard to keep the letters at bay, at the fringes of my consciousness. It galls me to admit that it's easier to put them out of my mind when I'm in Josh's house.

Easiest of all when I'm in his bed. What could possibly happen to me there? Josh's home might as well be a fortress. And the thickest, most impenetrable gate is the man himself. "He's just doing his job," I finish lamely.

Marlena purses her lips, cocking her head to the side. "I don't think so, Beth. I think there's more going on with him." A surprising note of sincerity colors her voice, washing away the tequila giggle. Her gaze sharpens. "I've met other guys like him. Before Scott." A flicker of emotion moves across her face too quickly for me to identify it. Sadness? Confusion? Impossible to pin it down. "You can't tell me you haven't noticed."

"Noticed what, exactly?" I fold my arms over my chest. Out on the dance floor my skin warmed to meet the air around us. Marlena and I had been in our own little bubble of heat and movement, with Josh and Scott hovering in our orbit. They kicked up the heat. Josh's eyes burned as much as his hands did. But now the sweat evaporates from the back of my neck. The resulting shiver peaks my nipples underneath the purple slip of a dress I borrowed from Marlena. The waiting ticks a few more valuable seconds off my life. *Say it. Just say it.*

"All that pain he carries around with him." She hugs herself too, the mirror image of me. "That's a guy who's seen some shit."

"Everybody's seen things." I make an effort to uncross my arms and stretch my wrists in front of me. Limber up. We'll be back on the dance floor where we belong soon enough.

"Mmm." Her eyes flick toward the mirror. "Not like this. He reminds me of..." Another flicker of unnameable emotion. I want to turn her face back toward me, but Marlena hesitates another moment before she does. "It doesn't matter. Just watch him when we go back out there. You'll see how he's keeping everybody at arm's length. He practically radiates a stay-the-fuck-away-from-me vibe."

I open my mouth to disagree. I've spent more time than I care to tally up telling him to fuck off. But Marlena's words make me reconsider all the times I've watched him move through a crowd. That night after the performance, in the lobby with Trevor Dunn. He'd put all those drinks in his arms and physically pushed him an inch backward. The rest of the people in that room didn't need that kind of nudge. I can see it in my mind's eye—the way the men and women in their stiff formal clothes had sensed him coming and moved out of the way. I'd been too annoyed to notice it then. And he'd been out of line.

"Right?" Marlena answers the expression on my face and the silence on my lips. "You know what I'm talking about. He's got a black hole inside of him. If you're not careful, you'll get sucked inside." She makes a twisting gesture in front of her own gut and clicks her tongue.

I force a laugh and reach out to pat her arm. "You're dramatic when you're drunk on tequila."

Marlena winks at me. "Maybe I'm dramatic. But maybe I'm right. And you know what happens with wounded men. Don't you, Beth?"

"Of course I know." But I don't—not really. Marlena is the one who plucks men out of the world around us and coaxes money from their pockets with a smile and a kiss. I'm the one who keeps my fists raised at all times. How could I do otherwise? Especially when it means ignoring the hard-won lessons I've spent my life learning. "Let's go dance."

Marlena leans over the sink and touches up her lipstick, a bold red color that will probably make Scott's eyes darken. "Just be careful." The lipstick disappears into her purse and her arm slides back into place, our elbows locked together. "Guys like that—they always self-destruct in the end. You don't want to be standing too close when it happens." She lets out a little sigh. "But damn, does he ever love watching you dance. Those pretty green eyes of his light up like the freaking aurora borealis. Don't tell him I noticed. He'd be mortified."

CHAPTER ELEVEN

*The first ballet on record was staged in the year
1581 by Catherine de' Medici, the queen of France.
She, the king, and her court also performed in it. It
was staged in the Louvre Palace in Paris lasting
nearly five hours.*

JOSH, FIVE YEARS AGO

WHEN YOU THROW pebbles at someone's
window, restraint is important.

Too hard and you'll break the glass, leading to
an unpleasant scenario—especially if there are
strict parents slumbering downstairs. I have some
experience with stealing pretty girls out of
bedroom windows.

Bethany makes me wait.

It takes three pebbles against the pane for her
shadow to appear at the glass. She lifts the sil and
pushes her head out. A smile flits across her face,
her teeth white in the moonlight, before she can
think to act cool around me. That smile makes

me puff up like a goddamn lion.

An object comes fluttering down and lands on the ground at my feet, taking shape as I pick it up. A messenger bag. Cloth, sturdy, a long strap. Bethany follows a moment later. She lands in a half-crouch, the movement appropriate for the stage. Anticipation thrums in the air around her. "Where are we going?"

"Wow. Not even a hello kiss for the man who's going to rock your world?"

Bethany makes a face. "So far, we haven't done anything except stand in the yard. Where are we going?"

"Somewhere you're going to like."

Skepticism shines from her expression. "How would you know what I like?"

"I was right about the beignets, wasn't I?"

Even in the moonlight I can see the flush of her skin. "Everyone likes beignets from Cafe du Monde. Try again."

I shouldn't, shouldn't, shouldn't—*shouldn't* be here, shouldn't be taking her out, shouldn't be giving in to this, whatever this feeling clawing through my veins is. But Bethany's made the second move. She climbed out the window. So I take her hand and twirl her under my arm. My dick throbs so hard it's at its limit. This goes much further and I'll have her twirling and twirling under my hands. *Mine.*

For tonight I'll pretend that this is simple. "There's a hint."

She comes to a graceful halt and lowers her heels to the ground, her eyes raking over my clothes. "I see. You want to get your hands on me." A flicker of a smile. "That's par for the course."

Bethany is still smiling when I get us to our destination, pulling my rental car into into a spot that's probably illegal, tucked into the end of an alley. She sits up straight in the passenger seat. "A back alley, huh? Very romantic."

"I never said anything about being romantic." She sticks close to my side when we get out. Smart. A nondescript metal door materializes out of the murky shadows at the side of the alley. "I said you'd like it." I can feel her holding her breath while I rap my fingers against the metal. The door cracks open, golden light pouring into the alley so thick I could run my fingers through it.

"Who's visiting?" The voice is cracked and smoky, almost worn through.

"It's me." The door swings open the rest of the way and I catch a glimpse of Bethany's face.

Lit like the sunrise. Bright and open. Nothing like the way she looked when I saw her in that warehouse. Any other girl would be terrified at the sight of the narrow death trap of a staircase and my asshole brain wonders if she knows this place. Knows other things, too.

At the bottom of the stairs the room opens out into a mass of bodies. Darkness descends, broken up by pulsing lights from the DJ station at the far end. This place has a reputation for relative safety. Dancing. Drinking. No bullshit. House music beats against my ears. Lucky for me, my time overseas stripped the most sensitive layers of my hearing, so it's bearable. "Do you want—" The question cuts itself off. Bethany's no longer beside me. She has already plunged into the crowd. My breath catches at the sight of her. She has so fully inhabited the music that it seems to be emanating from her, and the movements she makes—I recognize them. I've seen them once before. This is nothing like tightly scripted ballet. It's primal. A challenge.

An invitation.

The music wraps itself around my hips and pulls me forward with the same intensity as her dark eyes. There's no room for us to dance apart and no room for anyone else to touch her.

I take full advantage of it. Hands on her hips. On the back of her neck, where a sheen of sweat gathers. Her ass brushes against the front of my pants, teasing, and I'm ready to burst into flames. The fire engulfs me, becomes me.

Bethany hooks a hand around my neck and bares her throat to me.

I let my breath skim along her skin in place of my teeth.

"You want more of that." She breathes the accusation against my ear on the heels of a low laugh. "So even Joshua North needs a warm body."

"I'll let you in on a little secret. You think I'm the devil, but I'm human at the core."

"I don't believe it."

Her hip under my palm, her curves against my bones. "I've had feelings." The admission seems almost ridiculous in its simplicity. "I wasn't always a cold bastard. No—I was always a cold bastard. Just not this cold."

The energy around us, between us, shifts and changes. She keeps hold of me. Bethany's little T-shirt rides up, and she presses flesh against flesh. I can't get a full breath. The things I'd do to her if there were no clothes between us. If I could kick a door shut and flip the lock. Fuck the lock. Fuck the door, even.

"Feelings about what?"

Something snarky, on the edge of a lie, dies on the tip of my tongue. Truth blooms in its place. "I was pretty fucking pissed when my brother left for the army. For a while I thought I'd kill him myself if he ever came back." The old sense betrayal is like any of my other scars from bullets or knives or fists, only invisible. "He left us with our father." Who was a monster more terrifying than any I've met in the world—including traitors and bastards such as her brother. "And then I did the same thing to Elijah and came into my own as a piece of shit."

"Nobody could blame you for that," she murmurs into my ear.

But someone could. Elijah could. A cracking sensation at the center of my chest reminds me how much I miss them. "I blame myself for that. I'm a guilty motherfucker, sweetheart. I'm swimming in it."

"Swim somewhere else." Her body beckons. Bethany takes up space on the dance floor, her bends and turns forcing the world to recognize her existence. Push and pull, sway and dip. I won't let her get farther than an arm's length.

"Then they'd know." The truth is a thousand

stab wounds. What the ever-living fuck am I doing?

"Who'd know? And know what?"

"My brothers. They'd know that I care. Not that it matters, coming from a soulless monster." That truth feels casual. Comfortable. I have never been anything better than I am right now, but I'll be worse one day. Guaranteed. Bethany's eyes lock on mine, pools of darkness against the strobe lights. She's a fucking siren, drawing me off the edge of the ship. I could drown in the way she rolls her hips. Maybe I will, one day when she's not a one-way ticket to prison.

"Would it be so bad?" Her body moves against mine. The dance becomes sinuous and dark. "If they knew?"

"It would be fucking terrible if anyone knew." My heart thrashes against its bounds. "Getting close to people is a setup." It's an irony, because there's nothing separating us but sweat-slick clothes. It's a thousand degrees in here. A million. "You're a sucker if you think they'll do anything but leave you behind." Bethany rocks to one side, pulling us toward the edge of the crowd. On instinct I throw my weight back, keeping her here. But it only takes one lithe step for her to make her argument.

"I need some air," she says over the crushing bass. She doesn't lose contact with me all the way out to the alley. Outside, the dance doesn't stop. I can still feel the music under her skin. Bethany's eyes search mine. "Is that why you're buddy-buddy with my brother, then? Because you think he'll keep you around?"

My entire body bristles. "No," I growl. "Because when he finally gets what's coming to him, I won't give a fuck." I've said too much. She tenses beneath my hands. My muscles react for me, and I back her against the wall of the alley. There's the delicate line of her throat again, her pulse fluttering underneath. Exposed. One brush of my lips against her skin has Bethany panting.

"He's not all bad," she breathes. "You don't have to say things like that." Tension sings in her voice, but she doesn't push me away.

"Is that what you give a fuck about, sweetheart? Your brother?"

Her fists curl into my shirt. Starlight echoes in her eyes. "He's my brother. You care about your brothers. We're the same."

We're not the same. We're fucking not. She might have a preternatural grace and old understanding in her eyes, but she's as naive as they come. My nerves feel like live wires, exposed to the air and her touch. But no matter how raw they get, this will only ever be a false closeness. I can never, never let her in. Her or anybody else. The risks are too high. They'll always be too high. "We're not the same."

I can't let go of her. The cool night air swirls around us, making the hairs on the backs of my arms rise. One of her hands curls around my wrist. She holds tight to the bone. "I know what you need, Josh."

I can't say it out loud. I can only take it.

This time, when she kisses me back, it's hot and brave. It lands like a cannonball at the center of my soul. I pretend with all my might that there's something left for Bethany to destroy, but I'm already rubble.

BETHANY, PRESENT TIME

THE SOUND OF running water infiltrates my dream. It takes a period of time to realize that the water doesn't fit with the dream. I'm sitting in my high school math class, trying to get the numbers on the page in front of me to make sense. The *whoosh* of a shower, complete with the irregular splashes that suggest a person washing their hair, has nothing to do with an algebra test.

As soon as that thought is fully formed, the dream dissolves and I'm squarely back in the center of reality. Also known as Joshua North's personal bedroom. And his personal bed. I grab for the covers and pull them up to my neck. But...I'm fully clothed. Of course I am. He's made it abundantly clear that intimacy is not part of the deal.

Not that I expected intimacy from him. We stumbled into its gates on the first night, and he dragged us out and slammed them shut. I don't want that with him, anyway. I don't want any of this. Not the threatening letters. Not Landon's condescending treatment. He dismissed my opinions about this security team completely, and now look where it's gotten me.

In Josh's master suite, listening to him shower.

Unless a true apocalypse has happened, there can only be one man in the master suite's bathroom. He wouldn't have let anyone else walk into the bedroom. My mouth drops open. He walked past me, sleeping, to get to the en suite. Who does that? He does, obviously. Which means he doesn't really care that I'm sleeping in his bed. At the same time, he's ordered me to sleep *in his bed*. It doesn't add up.

When I came out of the dream, I was still tired. It took forever for me to fall asleep last night, yet again. Each time I woke up, the cycle started all over again.

Now I'm wide awake but frozen in the bed. He's in the shower.

I launch myself out of bed just to break the spell, then run my hands over my hair. I don't toss and turn much in my sleep. Years of ingrained habit. But what do I do now? Waltz into the bathroom and act like this is my home, too? I still haven't figured this part out. Josh would deserve it. He's the one who wouldn't stand for my apartment. The shower in the master suite is all modern tile with a big glass front. It takes up one entire wall of the bathroom. There's just no earthly way I can enter that space and not look in his direction. His naked, wet direction.

This isn't how I thought this would go. For one thing, I have class in a matter of hours. How many, I'm not sure. Where is my phone? I find it exactly where I left it on the bedside table, only it's been plugged into a charger.

He didn't want me out and about with a dead phone. At some point he came in here to plug it in so I wouldn't have to go without it. I'm not one of those people who spends a lot of time on my phone. Dancing takes up most of my waking hours.

What the hell is happening?

The other piece to this equation is that I suddenly and desperately have to pee. I probably could have held it off if I'd stayed in bed, but I'm upright, and gravity is a cruel mistress. Leaving this bedroom means I run the risk of Josh thinking I've disappeared. Staying means I run the risk of seeing him get out of the shower. Did he take all his clothes in there with him, or will he come out with a towel around his waist? Or no towel at all?

The phone tumbles onto the bed. I bury my face in my hands.

I'm not sixteen anymore.

I should not be acting like the man who's kicked down the door into my life and left it hanging from its hinges is anyone to get excited about. No. The only possible way forward is to carry on with what we now call our normal routine. This is the suite he's assigned me to, so that's the bathroom I'll use. I'll brush my teeth. I'll get dressed. I'll go to class. Noah, I'm sure, will be waiting to drive me.

Shoulders back, head up. This is not a dilemma.

I've just stepped around the first corner of the king-size bed when the water shuts off. The abrupt silence freezes me in place. Shit. *Shit.* The average time it takes a man to dry off his hard, muscled body is going to be nothing like the time it takes me to hastily scrub off excess water in a disgusting shared bathroom. I weigh the options—get caught as a living statue at the foot of the bed or the floor of the bathroom?

The deliberations have taken too much time.

Footsteps on bathroom tile. I lurch into motion and make it around to the other side of the bed. The bathroom door cracks open, tendrils of steam reaching out and brushing against my cheek. His eyes flare when he sees me. No smile graces his lips. "You're awake," he comments. "Good. Noah will be waiting out front to take you to the theater."

I'd expected a rush of heat after how long I spent pressing my thighs together underneath Josh's sheets last night. Instead he brushes by me surrounded by a deep freeze. A thick white towel only serves to highlight his nakedness. The muscles, the hair, the maleness of him.

"Fresh towels are in the linen closet, as always," he says over his shoulder on his way through the bedroom. I can't help but watch him go. He must know I'm looking. He walks with his shoulders set. Every step seems planned. God, even his back looks strong.

He almost makes it out the door without looking back. At the very last moment I catch a flash of emerald. Amusement flickers at his lips. He saw me check him out.

Then he's gone, the door shutting gently behind him.

CHAPTER TWELVE

*Forbidden from practicing any martial arts, slaves in
16th century Brazil developed Capoeira—fighting
disguised as athletic, impassioned dance.*

JOSH, PRESENT TIME

I'VE SPENT NIGHTS in the mountain cold
overseas.

I've pulled the trigger in life-or-death situa-
tions. I've hauled screaming men with bloodied
limbs and crazed eyes into helicopters. And now
I've done another torturous thing: walked past a
sleep-rumpled Bethany without touching her.

Sleeping with her is not on the fucking table.
It never has been, for a variety of reasons. Sleeping
near her doesn't seem to be an option, either.
Every time I doze off with her in the house, I fall
into vivid, filthy dreams involving the wide array
of ways her body could bend beneath mine. So
fuck sleep. I'll try again tomorrow.

I thought I could put those thoughts out of

my head. There was no way she was going to spend another night in that apartment, not even if I had to go and get her myself. That place might as well have been under a blinking neon sign that said OPEN FOR FUCKERY.

The way I feel right now, she's not any safer in my house.

I brace one arm against the wall of the walk-in closet and rip the towel from my waist. My dick stands at full attention. Jesus, if she walks in now, if that doorknob turns, I'll abandon the last shreds of self-control like the towel at my feet.

The doorknob stays put.

I can't work like this.

Protecting Bethany isn't some bullshit job that I can phone in. At North Security I don't get those kinds of assignments. That's not how we invest our time. I won't say this is personal. It can't be personal. Because letting myself get into that mind-set will get us both killed, or worse.

Sheer force of will isn't going to rid me of this erection.

She slept in a tank top last night. It was so fucking close to the one she wore that night I went to her house for the first time. That was a big fucking risk, throwing pebbles at her window. Her grandmother could have walked in. Her brother could have shown up at home. Anything could have happened. And instead I lured her out into the dark. It must've been a tough decision for her—go against me, or them? Give in to goodness or the rush of knowing that life is more complicated than following the rules?

I don't give a fuck about the rules right now. Not with my fist stroking hard and my teeth gritted to keep any sound from escaping. I'll never forget the sensation of her lips against mine. That first glancing kiss. The things her body can do. What they would do for me if I peeled off those leotards and the breezy skirts and bared her skin to me. All her skin. Every inch. All her most secret places. They would all be mine. Mine, mine, mine.

My release spills out onto the discarded towel. My dick jerks in my hand. For the first time since last night, my head is almost clear.

Footsteps pad on the carpet outside the door.

Fuck it. Let her come in. Let her see me like this. Let her see everything. My muscles brace for the light from the bedroom to hit me like a slap. For Bethany's wide-eyed gaze, no longer as innocent as it once was. Close. But not quite. She's seen things, I know she has. This would be something else entirely. It would explode the cool distance I've so far managed to build between us. A distance that, right now, seems very fragile.

The footsteps pause. My breath stops in my lungs.

Then the footfalls continue on, moving away until I can't hear them anymore.

BETHANY, PRESENT TIME

MAMERE LIVES IN a green house with a red door not far from the French Quarter. You can't see the Mississippi from her caved-in front porch, but you can smell it. You can smell everything from the tiny corner lot, including whatever the neighbors in the red house next door are cooking. Today it's jambalaya. Easy enough to tell by the sizzle of sausage in fat and the toasty bite of spices on the breeze. My mouth waters, but I don't so much as slow my step as I pass by Mamere's neon sign in the window. It still announces PSYCHIC READINGS in letters dull from age. A single tarot card decorates the corner of the window. A part of me is aware of the old swing in the back, where I used to wait for Josh. Most of me is dying to hear her voice.

Maybe he's thinking about that too. I don't ask him.

The porch creaks under our feet. I feel a flash of anxiety that Josh's solid weight might cause the whole thing to collapse. But no. It'll take more than one man to put an end to Mamere's house. It survived Katrina and it'll survive six feet of pure muscle, so long as he doesn't jump up and down on the old boards. He stands close enough behind me that I can feel where his body shapes the breeze. I've never thought of the porch as particularly large, but with him taking up all the available space, it's tiny.

Josh wouldn't let me come here alone. He let me get almost to the front door of his mansion before he detached himself from the shadows, spinning his car keys around one finger and whistling. Whistling. "I don't need a ride," I'd told him, drawing my bag in tight to my body. What I needed was five minutes without having to breathe him in. The most basic act of life is filled with him now. Every day. Every night. It's going to give me a heart attack.

Of course he gave me a withering look and told me to get in the car, *sweetheart*. I felt the space he kept between us like the sharp point of a knife. I shouldn't have been so quick to dismiss what Marlena said.

The red front door creaks open with the tinkle of the little shopkeeper's bell before I can knock.

A wrinkled grin splits Mamere's face. "I knew it was you, child. Come in, come in." Her eyes are almost completely white with cataracts. She shouldn't be able to see that it's me. It wouldn't be a stretch to believe she has some other sight. Especially when the smile falls away. Not quite a frown. "Ah," she says, lifting her chin in Josh's direction. "It's you. You're the one she dreams about." She presses her lips together, and I hold my breath. Heat crawls across my cheeks. I feel, rather than see, the smirk on Josh's face.

I should deny it, but the truth would be even more painfully obvious than it already is. Mamere isn't wrong. "Hi, Mamere." I step into the entryway of her house and let the burnt sage and incense engulf me. Her bones feel light beneath my arms. Smaller than I remember from the last time I saw her. But not frail. Still strong.

"Come sit. Both of you." She shuffles into the front parlor. I can't let myself relax—not with Josh standing here. Inside. How many times did I climb out to sneak away with him while Mamere snored down the hall? I force my thoughts away from those memories. I don't think Mamere can read my mind, even if she thinks she can. But why take the chance?

We settle into the antique chairs at the round table, and Mamere takes her seat across from us.

Josh seizes the opportunity to re-introduce himself. "Mrs. Lewis, I'm Joshua North." His voice heats up the air around us. I know he's not a good man, not some kind of golden boy you bring home to meet your parents, but the illusion is strong. "Bethany probably dreams about me because I'm an old friend of your grandson's."

I shoot him a look that has to be unmistakable disgust. What is he *doing*? I didn't bring him here to act like the two of them went to Yale together.

Mamere says nothing. She merely shuffles the worn cards of her tarot deck in her hands. This is our ritual. First, the cards. Then, the kitchen. The part that isn't going according to script is Joshua North sitting next to me on a chair that looks like it could crack under his solid muscles. It doesn't crack. The chair holds. I sink into the whirr and snap of her shuffling. We've entered into a sacred space, like the moment before the music starts in a performance. Mamere spreads the deck out in the center of the table, a wide fan. "Choose."

Joshua's smirk falters, but he doesn't look in my direction. "Me?"

"You." Mamere's lips form the word and settle back into a placid expression.

Josh hovers a hand over the deck. I read his palm once. Now I read the rough skin on the backs of his knuckles. The scar where his index finger meets his hand, so faded it's almost invisible. *Guys like that—they always self-destruct.* I wonder how quickly it can happen. Josh's hesitation is the barest moment, and then his finger comes down on a card. He tugs it out from the line. Mamere darts out a hand and turns it faceup.

We all stare down at it.

"Your granddaughter read my palm," Josh says into the silence, sounding almost cocky. "Does this card say the same thing?" The question is half addressed to me, half addressed to no one.

But I don't say a word. The backs of my hands tingle with a strange energy.

Mamere frowns at the card. The illustration is of a tower standing tall against a black, starless sky. A yellow bolt of lightning crashes into the top of the structure, sparks flying away from the point of impact. The Tower means danger. It means upheaval. It means destruction. My heart beats faster than the lightning strike depicted on the card, hitting its mark again and again in rapid succession. Mamere shifts in her seat. The doctors have said her vision is as good as gone, but she meets Josh's eyes anyway. "You've been living in this space a long time, haven't you?" She raps a knuckle on the center of the card. "Very much alone."

CHAPTER THIRTEEN

Dancer Raven Wilkinson was one of the first African American ballerinas permitted to join a ballet company. During the 1950s, she danced with the Ballets Russes de Monte Carlo under the condition that she pose as a white woman by painting her face.

JOSH, PRESENT TIME

"**N**O, NO, NO, Mamere. Let me make the tea." Bethany disengages the older woman's hand from the worn handle of the teapot with extreme gentleness and a laugh in her voice. "I came to visit you. I'll make the tea." In her grandmother's kitchen the rusty edge of her voice falls away. Afternoon sunlight spills over tea towels embroidered with the outline of a crystal ball. I can still smell the spices of dinners past. On any other day, it would make me want to take a seat at the table and eat until I was sated. I can't remember the last time I felt satisfied like that. Maybe never.

But today I want to get the hell out of here. That old woman's knuckle on the tarot card stopped my heart between beats. I'm not the kind of man who holds with cards and crystal balls, but she didn't need to tell me what that tower means. I felt the cold whisper at the pit of my gut. Same as when our dear old dad used to come home. You develop superhuman hearing when you live with a monster. A quarter-turn of the front doorknob was all it ever took to fill my veins with ice. One knock against that card, splayed on the table, had my defenses up. Bethany saw it—I know she did. Her eyebrows drew together. Her hand twitched as if to take mine. Unbelievable, that she would try to hold my hand when the truth was so evident, spoken aloud by Mamere.

Very much alone. Very much alone, crouched in the corner of my own closet. I give Liam shit about the baby bird. I use it as my own shield between me and what happened all those years ago. What's still happening inside my head. It didn't surprise me when Bethany's grandmother named her dreams. Bethany is an open book, with all her defiance and sadness and fight right there under the surface. But when she flipped that tower card to the table—Jesus. Gives me chills. And the only thing I hate more than being at the mercy of some old woman with a deck of cards is being at the mercy of surprises.

But leaning against the doorway in the kitchen, watching Bethany, I can't tear myself away.

I've never seen her in precisely this situation before. Her dark eyes are open, relaxed. She knows this choreography. It's worn into her very bones by years and years of focused practice. The set pieces, I can tell at a glance, always remain in the same position. It was like this when I'd come throw pebbles at the window. Mamere must have been losing her vision even then. Keeping the house this way let her hide it for longer. She never seems to hesitate. Even now she throws her hands up and laughs. "Why not let me make the tea? You're the one with places to go and the weight of the world on your shoulders, child."

Bethany shrugs off that metaphorical weight with a toss of her head. "I'm light as a bird."

A wizened hand drops onto her shoulder. "For a person so light, you're holding tight to that teapot. Is it keeping you on the ground?"

Bethany stops filling it in the sink and holds it daintily by her fingertips, raising her left hand to give the movement a playful flourish. "Better?" Her teasing is an arrow through the heart. A shock. A lightning bolt. Her laugh is a familiar soprano that fits in with the melody of this house. With her grandmother's low, echoing rumble of pleasure. It's so fucking domestic I could die.

This is what she'd be like as a wife. As a mother.

My throat constricts.

Someone else's wife.

I leave her in the kitchen and wander through the house, to the very back. This space started out as a porch. Somewhere along the life of the house it became a back room, closed in with panes of glass. The original wooden posts have become part of the wall. The floor feels less substantial under my feet. It's a step down from the rest of the house. But the floor isn't what captures my attention. The swing does.

It's a rickety, falling-down jumble of what used to be called play equipment. The swing still hangs from its chains. Someone as featherlight as Bethany might be able to sit on it still, but it would be a risk. The thing looks like the slightest breeze could bring it down. I used to plant my feet next to it and take aim at Bethany's window. A far fucking cry from taking aim at a shadow overseas, but the same adrenaline rush. Her silhouette started out the same way every other enemy's did. A barely visible outline against pitch darkness. Damn, did she become something different in the light. My dick goes hard at the memory of her muscles working in the climb. In the dance. *I know what you need, Josh.*

Her voice wraps around me like a rope and pulls me back to the kitchen. The teapot whistles on the stove. Bethany's set out three mismatched mugs on the countertop. She bows her head, a slight smile on her face. "—my own choreography." Mamere watches with rapt attention. It should be some Cinderella shit—the ever-suffering servant laying the teabags over the edges of the mugs. Balancing the strings just so. But I'm struck again, like a two-by-four to the back of the head, by the deep knowledge that she could be on her knees at the foot of my bed, naked and panting and begging, and still be a queen.

I'm one filthy motherfucker.

And for the next several moments, while Bethany goes on about studio space and a hundred other hopeful plans for the future that are like knives thrown into the hidden parts of me, I remain the filthiest motherfucker in this old house.

A knock at the door.

Bethany and her mamere lift their heads like a pair of birds, but it's me who goes to answer it.

Automatically. Like this is my house.

"Why would you want to do that?" Mamere says with a faint scoff. "It's as good as taking your clothes off for all those men."

A beat of silence. "I would have the final say." Bethany's voice is fierce but still gentle. Love suffuses every word. Forgiveness, even though each syllable is also ringed with pain. "Nobody would be telling me what to do. I would be in charge of the piece. I only need one chance to prove it."

I'm under no illusion that I could belong here. I don't entertain that ridiculous fantasy for a second. A man like me, part of something like this? Never.

Maybe I was entertaining that daydream, because something falls to the floor and shatters when I reach the door. Or perhaps that was only my complacency. Every nerve jumps into action. Why didn't I see this coming? Did I let her distract me? I fucking did. I was so busy watching her ass sway in her black leggings and imagining pulling them off with my teeth to take in the necessary details. Like the photos of Caleb Lewis that grace the walls in the entryway. Mamere keeps recent photos. Recent enough that what I did to Caleb shows on his face in one of them.

But I don't need a photo to know what he looks like now.

Because he's standing on the porch, his hands in his pockets.

There's a single heartbeat left where he doesn't see me. Caleb's not expecting me here, the fucker. I can't believe it. He should be on the lookout for me everywhere he goes. Then he lifts his head. Narrows his eyes. Scowls.

I fling the door open wide. "Welcome home, buddy."

He steps in and crushes my hand in his. "What the fuck are you doing here?"

I pound his back hard, pulling him close. I want him off-balance. "I'm at work," I tell him jovially. "Protecting a client."

"What client?" He backs up, putting some space between us, eyes ablaze. "What fucking client?"

"Caleb, come in here and have some tea." Mamere's voice floats out from the kitchen, knocking us apart as surely as if she'd stood between us and put her hands on our chests. Caleb still bristles, his shoulders set. What the hell does he think he's going to do, tackle me in front of his grandmother? No. He won't do that. "Bring your friend with you."

I snort back a laugh. "Yes, Caleb. Let's have some tea and catch up." I fix him with a wide grin that feels like a feral dog baring its teeth.

"I'm short on time." He turns on his heel and goes into the kitchen. I follow him in time to see him wrapping up Mamere in his big arms. After all the things I've seen him do, it's jarring to see him hug her so carefully. We're all such fucking contradictions, aren't we? "I can't stay," he tells her, though he was clearly planning to stay when he got here. He was wearing that half-relieved, half-contemplative expression we all wear when we're thirty seconds from kicking our feet up and closing our eyes somewhere safe. Caleb should know better. Nowhere is safe.

"Bethy's put out the tea," Mamere protests. She runs her hands over the front of his shirt. "It won't take you a minute to drink it."

Caleb keeps his body angled away from Bethany as much as he can. She presses herself against the counter. I can tell she's trying to make it look like a casual lean. It's not working. I keep my posture relaxed. It's no reflection of how I feel, which is like a mean German shepherd at the end of its chain. I want to throw myself between them. Caleb straightens up and heads back toward the door, caught between the two of us. The air in the room crackles. His right hand balls into a fist. I track every twitch of his muscles. I let my guard down walking in here like a fucking idiot. It won't happen again.

"Stay," says the old woman. Bethany's face is blank. She's focused on some spot in the middle distance, far from here. She holds herself tight as if she's trapped between wanting to run and wanting to stand tall. Like there's some part of her that still, after all this time and all this bullshit, wants to lean into Caleb and face the world with him. It turns my stomach.

"I've got some things to take care of," Caleb insists. "I'll come back another time." For the first time since he walked in, he swings his gaze from me to Bethany and back. Caleb Lewis doesn't dare sneer at me in front of his grandmother, cataracts in her eyes or not. "As for you two." The threat rings like a bell in the center of this cocoon of a kitchen. Mamere blinks, her near-blind eyes tracking Caleb's voice. "I'll be seeing you both very soon. Consider that a promise."

BETHANY, PRESENT TIME

SLEEPING IN JOSH'S bed is killing me.

It's only been a week, and it's a good bed.

Joshua North wouldn't buy a piece of shit for a bed. It's not some secondhand thing dragged in off the curb or even an IKEA piece that looked good in the showroom but deteriorates by the day under the fitted sheet. It's somehow both plush and firm—probably the nicest mattress I've ever slept on in my life. And it's making me feel like a broken doll.

I add a bit of extra stretch into my third position, and then my fourth. My shoulders are tight knots that won't release. I can feel others knots in my hamstrings. My body is a mass of scar tissue and tension.

I'm not sleeping next to him every night, feeling the security of his even breath next to me. I'm sleeping alone, but his scent is everywhere. My nose should be used to it by now. I shouldn't be drowning in desire every time I suck in a breath.

Folding down the sheets doesn't do anything to stop it.

Kicking off the blankets only forces me to pull them back up.

And all night, every night, I can feel him sitting out there.

Guarding. Watching. And for what? Nothing has happened since he pushed his way back into

143

my life and set up camp. Not so much as a threatening sticky note.

Landon claps his hands, and I wrench my thoughts away from that damned bed and move into position at the center of the floor.

Rehearsal should take my mind off him. It doesn't.

Every single morning, I come here hoping to lose myself in the steps and turns and bends. And every single morning, I spend all of practice fighting with my own brain. It wants to follow Josh out to where he sits in the hallway. It wants to study his shadow through the frosted glass of the studio door.

It wants, it wants, it wants.

It would help if I actually liked what I'm practicing. We do a few run throughs of Olivia Twist each morning to stay fresh for our performances at night, but the challenging work is on the new piece. Next season we'll be debuting a show called Duckling, a modern, abstract retelling of the Ugly Duckling.

Landon cast me in the lead role. Even in a small troupe such as this, it isn't something I should take for granted. There are a few reasons why I'm uncomfortable…

1) Landon keeps interrupting to change the

choreography, making it more and more elabo-
rate, more and more unnatural for the human
body. Dance should expand what we're capable
of, not contort us to prove we can.

2) He also keeps standing in for Marlena,
who's playing the mother duck, supposedly to
show us the steps correctly, which means I've had
his hands all over my body, in places a mama
duck's hand would never need to be.

3) The dark-toned duckling who turns into a
beautiful white swan has unfortunate racial
overtones when played by a person, especially in
light of the costuming he plans. He's even asked
for my makeup to be darker in the opening,
lighter in the reveal.

The music starts, leaping into the first movement of the piece, and I jump in exactly on point,
making my arms flutter in dramatic, duck-like
fashion that feels uncomfortable and looks even
worse. I will not let the struggle show on my face.

Marlena moves by in a blur, her worried eyes
the only feature that stands out.

I lengthen my neck. I buckle down. And I
whirl straight into Landon, who's planted himself
in the center of the practice floor, hands on his
slender hips.

He grabs my elbow at the same time his shout

to stop the music registers. It's a cymbal crash to the side of my head, loud and reverberating. His fingers squeeze the flesh of my arm and on instinct I shake him off. "Landon, what the—"

He mutters low and close to my ear. "It looks ridiculous."

Shock coats me in a thick layer of embarrassment. What the hell is he thinking, grabbing me like this? They're his steps, his beats. "I'm sorry. I'll try it again."

"Don't apologize," Marlena says, her voice sharp. "You haven't done anything wrong. That's how it's written in the notes."

His face looks redder than I've seen it, and it occurs to me that he's humiliated by his own choreography. "You're not doing it the way I want. We've been working on this for weeks and you're acting like a first-year student in a state college."

The blows land one after the other. I want to put a hand over my gut to protect myself. It's too late. The pain is already there, blooming through my stomach. It's a not-so-subtle reminder that he went to Tisch, even if he didn't graduate. I don't have a single college credit to my name. I went directly to work an acrobatic show in Vegas, where I was recruited by Cirque du Monde. It's not a bad pedigree, as dancing goes. There are plenty of dancers who would want that opportunity, but it's not the same as the professors and the degrees.

This is a portion of the dance I've been meaning to talk to Landon about. A simple adjustment to the steps could make them flow so much better. Not just for me, for everybody. My breath comes fast and harsh. The words in my mind are a jumble.

"Listen." I find myself leaning in, trying to put on a smile, like Landon and I are on the same team. We should be on the same team, damn it. "I've been thinking about that eighth beat. There's this transition that keeps popping into my head, and I thought maybe it would look great." I show the new transition to illustrate my words. It gets rid of this awkward, unintentional jostle we have to do, trying to make a theoretical idea into something that real bodies do. It's athletic and graceful, but also real.

Landon cocks his head to the side, a pretend expression of exasperation on his face, though it doesn't hide his meanness. "Do you have a question about how it's supposed to look, Bethany? All you had to do was ask."

My cheeks heat. He's making it sound like I

don't understand the steps. I could do them in my sleep. That's not the issue. "No... I'm sorry. Maybe I'm overstepping."

"Overstepping?" He gives a short, hard laugh. "You are the dancer, right? I'm the choreographer. How about you focus on your feet."

Marlena looks pale, her lips tight with anger or shock.

Anger. Shame. Anger. Shame. My feelings circle them both, unable to land. "No, you're right. It's not my job. I just thought that maybe the flow would—"

"The flow does what, exactly? You think you can make it better with your cute little changes to the steps?" He sounds incredulous. Mortified heat burns me from the top of my head to the tips of my shoes.

"Maybe," I whisper, hating myself and hating him.

"Get this straight." A finger points at me, and I flinch back. I hate myself for it. "I'm the director. You're just moving parts. Keep your opinions to yourself and get your ass in order before you ruin another run-through. Got it?"

"Got it," I whisper. My throat closes up, tears burning at the corners of my eyes. I will not let them fall. I will. Not. Let. Them. Fall. He could break my legs in front of everyone. Better that than this.

The dead silence in the studio has taken on a character of its own. It feels like poison ivy. It feels like shame. The same searing shame as when the woman at the food bank in the church basement pursed her lips and told me that I'd overfilled my bag. I'd taken too fucking much. Gotten too big for my food bank britches, even while my stomach ate itself for survival. She made me put the box of noodles back.

I want to melt into a puddle on the floor, but somehow I make it through the rest of practice. Landon's words echo in my head. Just moving parts. I'm a puppet on a string. I'm as good as a prostitute. It's a sick sort of validation. I've been right all along. They only want me for the meat on my bones. Everybody, from Mamere on down, thinks this is it for me. *Twirl and dance, little doll. There's nothing else for you.* Who needs a brain when you can let your arms hang in first position and the master will make the moves?

Failure. I'm a failure. I've kept myself off the street through literal blood and sweat, and the world still wants to slap me into line.

Wrenching open my locker with all my strength feels good. Right. Like I could rip it off its hinges, and the locker would deserve it.

And then I see the letter.

I actually feel the blood drain from my face. My first instinct is to squeeze my eyes shut and see if it goes away. No. It's still there. My hand trembles on the metal lip of the locker door. The others came in envelopes, through the mail. This came hand delivered. Under any other circumstance, I might find it almost adorable. The letter is rolled into a small scroll. It's attached to a flower.

A dead flower.

A flower that's been dead for some time. It's the dried-out husk of what once was a tulip. The brittle edge of the petal feels sharp enough to cut my finger, but of course it doesn't. Wait, what am I doing? I shouldn't be touching it. But I already did. I've already made one mistake. One mistake in a long series of mistakes, beginning back in childhood, when I got the stupid idea that I matter for more than my body.

Since I've already touched the flower, I shove the whole nasty bundle into my backpack.

Out at the curb, Noah waits in one of North Security's black SUVs. He scrambles from the front seat to open the back door when he sees me coming. "Class let out early?" His eyes hold a cautious curiosity.

"Yes. I need to go home."

This is not the whole truth. What I need to do is go to a real home. A home that doesn't smell like Joshua North. A home that doesn't tie knots into my muscles and keep me awake at night. But I can't do that, can I? It was one thing to be reckless when I thought the letters were idle threats. An unwell individual having twisted fun. A letter in my locker feels dangerous on a deep, awful level. Someone had to stand in the hall while I was in class. Someone had to look at my things. Someone had to carefully place the flower on my backpack so it would be at eye level when I opened the locker door. And all this—all the guarding, all the sleepless nights—has done exactly nothing to prevent it.

Back at the pink mansion, of which every inch belongs to Joshua North and no part belongs to me, I stalk into his office. Anger has overtaken the fear, bubbling in my veins like poison champagne. I wrestle the flower out of my bag. Josh heard me coming. He always does. He sits behind his desk in an attitude of casual waiting. It's bullshit, and I know it.

I let the flower fall from my fingertips.

"What the hell is that?" He's on his feet, leaning over the desk, emerald eyes boring into mine. "Was this in the mail?"

"No. In my locker." It's his fault. I want to blame it on him so badly.

Naked fear flashes through his eyes like heat lightning. "Fuck, Bethany. Did you say anything to Noah?" His voice is a boom of thunder. The storm is directly above us. No time to take cover. "Did you tell him about this on the way?"

"No." I sound petulant. Small. I don't care.

Josh's phone looks like a fragile sheet of glass in his hand. Actually, that's what it is. The fact that he hasn't shattered it by the force of his grip is astonishing. He presses it to his ear. "I need you back at the studio. He left something in her locker. Yes. A flower, and another one of the fucking letters. Search the whole place. Shut it down." The phone falls to the table next to the flower with a clatter. Josh doesn't even flinch. "That's not a regular tulip. What kind of flower is it?"

"What does it matter?" I roll my eyes. I'm going back in time. I'm sixteen again, only worse than when I was sixteen. So much worse. When I was sixteen, Joshua North couldn't help but kiss me in the alley outside the dance club. Now he's got his knuckles pressed down on his desk. So much restraint. What a good guy. He glares at me. "It's a tulip. Don't you recognize tulips?"

"Can't say that identifying flowers has been a big part of my job description. I've been too busy putting down threats to our national security."

"Oh, wow." My voice sounds tight with tears and rage. I hate that too. "Is that why you thought you could take over my entire life? Because you're so good at killing people? You're not exactly acing this job, I hope you know."

He draws himself to his full height. Josh towers over me, his shirt straining over his muscles. "You need to go into the bedroom until I have a handle on this situation. That's the most secure place. I'll post someone outside the door."

"Fuck you," I spit. "I'm not hiding in your bedroom any longer. It hasn't done any good. Clearly."

He brings a hand down hard on the surface of his desk, the impact vibrating the room. "Damn it, Bethany, I wasn't the one at the studio today. If it was me—"

"If it was you *what*?" My voice breaches the last boundary. I try so damn hard not to fly off the handle. I try so hard to look like the woman I have to be in order to claw my way up the ranks in my career. Docile. Agreeable. But this stress feels like it could shatter my bones. "You wouldn't have seen him drop off the letter, either. You'd be too busy staring at my ass while I danced like I'm a piece of meat. Just admit it."

"No," he growls.

"Just admit it," I hiss between gritted teeth. My backpack falls to the floor. I'm leaning over his desk, a bare inch between us. "You like the way I look in a leotard. You get off on keeping me locked up in your bedroom, where no other man can touch me. You're just like Caleb. All you ever wanted is to keep everybody else's greedy fingers off me, like you *own me*—"

Who reaches first? Him or me? The next words out of my mouth are cut off by Josh's fist digging into the front of my leotard. Yanking me toward him. My hip bumps the front of the desk. The fabric holds. It's stronger than it looks. His breath is hot on my lips. Jaw set. The gold ring around his pupils is a tiny flame at the center of cut emeralds. Somehow my own hands are fisted in his shirt. Which of us is pushing? Which of us is pulling?

"You." He forces the word through the hard set of his jaw.

And then he snaps.

His mouth crashes into mine the moment he

hauls me over the desk. One knee knocks an agate paperweight to the floor. I'll have a bruise there later. Good. Let there be evidence of his need. His lips demand everything from me. He kisses the corner of my mouth and scrapes his teeth over my bottom lip. He has me in an iron grip. Like he might not ever let go. I'm molten beneath kisses so rough and so tender that they steal the air from my lungs. My thighs tremble from the position, from the fear, from the fact that I practiced hard. I'm dying for him to touch me there. Dying. A deafening heartbeat fills the room—his or mine, I don't know.

We're almost matched in height this way, with me kneeling on the desk. I'm tall enough to clutch at his shirt. I can use my weight as a counterbalance. But I'm still the one on my knees.

CHAPTER FOURTEEN

Tchaikovsky's Swan Lake premiered in Moscow in 1877. Critics dismissed it as too noisy and too symphonic. Only after a revival and re-choreography in 1895 did the ballet become a widespread success.

JOSH, PRESENT TIME

GIVE IN, GIVE in, give in. The only thing I've ever wanted is to give in.

What is the purpose of denial?

Bethany claws frantically at the front of my shirt, her fingernails digging in hard beneath the fabric. She tastes so fucking sweet. Her lips are puffy and red almost immediately, and I lick her bottom lip to taste her again. She tips her head back and welcomes my tongue into her mouth. Her entire body is a taut line. It can't be easy to balance herself on her knees on the slick surface of my desk. Her muscles hold her in place. Her toes dig in. What I wouldn't fucking give to see those toes curl in a real release. But I'll take the battle for now. Of course I'll fucking take it.

Years. *Years* are pent up in this kiss. Years of wanting and waiting and a twisted desire to make her do the filthiest things. That pure, graceful body in those pure, graceful clothes. I'm hard as a rock. Harder than a rock. I'm hard as rough diamonds hewn from the mines. I never wanted her to come easy. I got my fucking wish. She's a wildcat.

I slip a hand behind her neck. Her skin mists with sweat. I know better than to think she's still in a state from her practice. Bethany dances hard. She recovers quickly. This is from me. I'm doing this to her. Her perfect bun fits into the notch at my thumb like it was meant to be there.

Her hips roll forward. The new contact makes my dick leap. I'm going to fucking come in my pants, that's what's going to happen. Every muscle is tight with need for her. I want to push inside her and take up all the available space. I want to pin her beneath me so she has nothing left to do but writhe against my sheets. I want to fuck her so hard and for so long that her perfect bun is left in ruins.

A groan escapes me. I've been playing mind games for too fucking long now. Longer than the week she's lived in my house. She's the game.

Think about Bethany Lewis and I lose. I saw her name on that list for North Security and I've been losing every second since. Now it's clear, crystal fucking clear, that behind the closed door of my bedroom she's been thinking the same thoughts.

We're the same.

We're still not the same. But this animal desire isn't just me. It pours off Bethany in waves. She bites at my lip, exchanging one scrape of teeth for another. Her nails work their way into the back of my neck, up to where I keep my hair in a crisp line. That's a habit that will last the rest of my life. So will the taste of Bethany on my tongue.

She makes a little noise in the back of her throat. Her knees inch apart on the desk.

Fuck, I want it.

I could pull her off the desk right now. I could bend her soft, pliable body with its lean, hard muscles over the unforgiving wood and pin her there. She would hate it or she would love it, but she would beg for more either way. I allow myself another taste of the seam of her lips. Memorize the way they part for me. The strap of her leotard lies in a perfect fit against her skin. I push one finger beneath it. I trace it down to the neckline, down to the cleft between her breasts.

Her small, tight, beautiful breasts. They rise. They fall.

Her dark eyes snap open and meet mine.

Fuck.

I'm the devil on earth. I was the devil's son, but I've become him now. Monstrous as I am, I can't ignore the fear I see in her eyes. Like two flickering candles. Unmistakable. Regret roils through every inch of me, tidal in its power.

Hands on either side of her face, cupping the line of her neck. She's delicate as a bird at the juncture where her pulse meets her jawbone. Bethany relaxes. She thinks I'm going to pull her in for more. I know it from her hungry sigh. As if she hasn't had enough to eat all her life. For once, we're not prodding at the other's open wounds. We're pulling together.

And I have to push her away.

It hurts me to do it. To create that extra space between us. Bethany's face falls into confusion. "Why?" she breathes. The question is enough to make me bleed out, the life pumping out of me onto my polished hardwood floors.

"Not tonight."

Whatever this is, whatever it could become—it can't be tonight. She's fucking terrified. She's throwing herself at me out of abject fear. A man stalked her at the studio, where she should have been safe. Where Noah should have been watching. I'll have to post someone outside the studio, if I ever let her go back. I'm a filthy, depraved motherfucker with ragged shreds of a soul, but I can't take advantage of Bethany like this.

She sinks onto the desk, her polyester practice skirt in no-nonsense black pooling around her thighs. Her chin sinks toward her chest. My heart tears out of mine. I want to lower her to the desk and spread her legs. My dick demands it. Instead I lift her in my arms.

Dancers are not insubstantial people. They look that way, from the rows of seats in a theater, but it's an illusion. Bethany's petite frame is girded by the hard muscles necessary to propel her into the air and break her fall on the way down. She's strong in a way that most people can only dream of. But she still feels light in my arms. It takes no effort to whisk her out of my office and up the grand staircase. Five steps in she rests her head against my chest.

In the master bathroom I turn the shower on. The hiss of the water fills the room with a soothing white noise. She walked out of practice without showering, and I know she hates that feeling. It's my life's greatest sacrifice to keep my eyes in appropriate places while I strip her out of her sweat-soaked leotard and slip her shower cap over her hair. While she showers, I force myself to collect her favorite pajamas—the ones I've seen her in the most. Teal, with a pattern of hearts around the hem. I push the switch on the lamp next to the bed. The light glowing from under the lampshade gives the bedroom a more stately quality. Like I don't still want to destroy her on this mattress, on these sheets.

When the shower shuts off, I wait a small eternity and knock on the door. It cracks open, and Bethany blinks out at me. "Yes?"

"Clothes."

She takes them and seals herself off again, emerging ten minutes later with no shower cap and a tired droop to her shoulders. Bethany doesn't fight me when I take her hand. She lets me lead her to the bed and help her in. Everything she does is imbued with a natural grace, including lowering her head to the pillow. One hand slips beneath the edge of the pillow. Her eyes flutter shut.

I feel too big for the room to contain me. The blood in my body feels too raucous to be contained by my own flesh. My heart is an army on the march. It'll take an act of God to stop it. But all it takes to tuck her in is a lift of the blankets. I smooth them down over her shoulders. Safe and sound. Like a child.

Her eyes follow me when I step back from the bed. When did she start watching me? Bethany swallows. "You said not tonight."

One step and I'm close enough to skim my hand over her hair. Her eyelids flutter shut at my touch. It's fucking inconceivable, that anyone could get any semblance of comfort from me. So inconceivable that it breaks something loose in my chest. Something I almost never give. I'm not the kind of man who makes promises. Promises are almost always a bad bet. But one of them rolls off my tongue anyway. "If you still want me tomorrow," I swear fervently, "I'll do it. Whatever you want."

Just before she falls asleep, I see the ghost of a smile on Bethany's lips.

CHAPTER FIFTEEN

Adelina Patti was the highest paid soprano of her time. She made her debut as a child in New York and sang at Covent Garden for twenty-five seasons. When asked for her rates to perform, the theater manager replied, "Why, Madame, that is four times as much as we pay the President of the United States for a full year." Patti replied, "Well, then, why don't you get the President to sing for you?"

JOSH, FIVE YEARS AGO

MUD SUCKS MY boots another inch into the swamp. Caleb's idea of a celebration was to come out to Blind Lagoon two hours before sunset and shoot as many ducks as possible. Out on the bayou, everything is waterlogged and the scent of rot sits heavy on the surface of the water. Cypress trees loom in the light. The sun sinks below the horizon in barely perceptible increments.

My gut is unsettled in this heat. Congratulations to Noah and me. We're part of Caleb's gang now, and we came here to seal our agreement in the blood of dead ducks.

If we can manage to shoot any.

Something's off about the trip. Everybody knows duck hunting's better in the morning, but here we are, with the remains of a case of beer and a haphazard collection of waders and boots. It's a parody of a group of friends.

It's a half-hour drive from the city to Blind Lagoon. Caleb's Jeep is parked half a mile behind us at a nondescript parking area off highway 90. Connor and Noah were both buzzed when they tipped the aluminum boat into the first available shadows. Connor, obnoxious and loud. Noah, silent as always. He never says a fucking thing, that guy. If I could get him alone, I could get a better idea of what he's about. But being alone with a guy whose former partner met an unfortunate end isn't high on my agenda tonight. Or ever.

"We've got a system, okay?" Connor shouts at full volume.

He's such a fucking asshole. Yes, we're out in the middle of nowhere—but it's not like we've fallen off the map. If we can get here, so can anybody else.

"Nobody counts a goddamn thing in the army. They say they do, but why do you think Uncle Sam gives them. unlimited credit? It's because all kinds of bullshit slip through the cracks. Well, we've found one of the cracks. Lucrative as fuck. A gun here, a gun there. Soon you've got enough to sell on the black market. We get deployed, it gets easier. Who the hell is paying attention to that stuff when you've got the Taliban breathing down your neck? Nobody." He slings his Remington across his back and cracks open another can of the shittiest beer known to mankind. His gulps are loud enough to make a squirrel nearby screech itself into action and get the fuck away from us. Connor crushes the can in his fist, tips his head back, and howls.

"Shut the fuck up." Caleb shoves the boat up onto a rise in the ground. We used it to get over some of the deeper parts of the swamp. The damn thing can barely stay above water. Sets my teeth on edge. "You're going to scare the ducks away." His eyes linger on me when he turns around and lifts his gun out of the bottom of the boat.

"Sorry, boss." Connor pastes on a shit-eating grin. "Just trying to bring the boys up to speed. Things are happening, if you know what I mean."

Caleb smirks. "You think we're going to be

smuggling anything out here in the damn swamp? They'll learn on the job. Settle the fuck down and shoot some ducks."

He checks his ammo.

I pretend to take another swig of beer. There's not a chance in hell I'm actually going to drink out here, away from witnesses. I can feel Caleb's eyes tracking me and make sure to make the next swallow obvious. He doesn't trust me completely. Not yet. I'm still the new guy. It's a sensible way to do business.

I don't trust him at all. Honestly, I won't be shocked if this ends with a bullet in my back and a quick descent to the bottom of the swamp. I wouldn't be the first guy to go out that way. Bodies have a way of disappearing in the bayou. Some of them resurface in parts. Some of them never resurface at all.

My one pang of regret is that I didn't go and see Bethany before this boys' night out. It makes no fucking sense, because she's not mine.

I aim my gun to the horizon. A movement in the brush. A duck flies through the trees. It's right between my crosshairs… I move an inch to the right and pull the trigger. A loud blast. The duck flies away. "Damn," I say, my voice flat.

"Nice try," Caleb says, sounding smug.

He wants to be the best shot here. I could say that's why I missed on purpose, but the truth is, I don't have the heart for killing at the moment. I'm sick and fucking tired of it. Maybe that's why I agreed to it when my commander sat me down with someone from the CIA. *We've been looking into Caleb Lewis. You're in a unique position to get information for us. There's a commendation in it for you. And if you're interested, a job with us.* Who exactly are you? That's what I asked. *Get the information. Then we'll talk.* So who the fuck knows? Someone who gathers information instead of dodging bombs in the middle of the fucking desert, so yeah, I'm interested.

A fly buzzes by my ear, and I swat it away. Water sloshes against Caleb's boots. He stands shoulder to shoulder with me. How far is he going to take this? Is he going to sling an arm around my shoulders and welcome me into the fold?

Jesus. I'm not sure I'll be able to fake my enthusiasm if he does.

"Connor's right." He trains his gun out over the surface of the water and looks through the scope. "We've got a good fucking system. And at our level, very few people are paying attention. They underestimate us, don't they?"

Caleb thinks we're all just above grunts.

We've got enough access to get to the weaponry, and he's scraped together enough trust to rob the United States Army blind.

Noah wades past us, a wad of chew in his cheek. He wades a respectable distance before he spits into the water at his feet. Caleb and I shift forward to get in a line with him. Better this way. If one of them is going to shoot me tonight, I'll see it coming. Not that it'll make any difference. I think about Bethany's smile, flashing white in the starlit darkness of her grandmother's backyard. I wonder if she knows where I am tonight. If she'll think anything of it if I don't come back. Morbid shit.

"It'll be more lucrative now that you're on board," Caleb adds.

"Good. I'm not going to help you out of the fucking kindness of my heart."

A chuckle. "Kindness of your heart. That's a good one, North."

Caleb is right about that. I had the last vestiges of kindness beaten out of me years before I shipped off to boot camp. It almost made me feel sorry for some of the guys who signed on at the same time. They were soft. Came from suburbs named after Robin Hood fairy tales. Flinched away from a punch.

My older brother walked away without looking back. A year later I did the same thing. I haven't spoken to either of them since then. For once I wish that I'd changed that. I'd like their advice about this. Does it make me a fucking snitch to turn on Caleb? Do I even want a job that's based on those lack of principles?

Then again, those guns he's selling will be used against me. Against my older brother Liam. Against Elijah too, if he enlisted the year he turned eighteen.

That's reason enough to turn on him.

Except his sister is Bethany.

Dear Liam and Elijah, how would you feel about your dear brother turning traitor just so he can properly fuck a sixteen year old girl? Not exactly a sweet family reunion, but one that's fitting for the North family.

Noah pulls the trigger of his 12-gauge so smooth and quick the click barely registers before the shot rings out. I stand tall, my own gun still hanging from the strap across my back. A line of ducks rises from the water in a panic. Wings pumping. Sounding the alarm to one another. I have the wild hope that it's not too late for them.

Or maybe it's me I'm thinking about.

"Got one," says Noah. It's a typical Noah

comment. Brief.

"Fuck yes," Connor shouts.

He takes aim at the fleeing ducks and squeezes off three shots that go so wide I have half a mind to scold him about wasting shells.

I keep my damn mouth shut.

Noah sloshes out to get his kill. He slings it into a shopping basket in the bottom of the boat. It's my turn to casually get my gun in my hands and flick off the safety. I don't like the way Caleb's looking at me. Makes the hairs on the back of my neck reach for the sky. Does he know I've been taking Bethany out? Is that what this shit is all about? I'm not stupid enough to think that Caleb has any depth of goodness left in him. But he does have a certain lust for blood and vengeance. We all do. Thank you to the army for making it a marketable skill.

The minutes bleed away, the sun wheeling toward the tops of the cypress trees. I've successfully pretended to drink the same can of beer for the entire outing. The color leeches from the bayou while the seconds tick by. Frogs sing louder. I count my own heartbeats. Each one is a small triumph. Noah shoots another duck. Caleb lurks around, looking smug as hell. I keep my finger off the trigger…but close by. Somehow it doesn't seem like a good bet to waste a shot on a harmless duck. Easy enough to play up feeling buzzed. Caleb stops watching me quite as close.

By the time Caleb flicks on the light at the front of the aluminum boat, the air is thick with flies. Connor's drunk. The light catches his eyes and reflects back an almost crazed excitement. It's too much for a duck hunting trip during which he's killed zero ducks.

Something's not right.

Either that or I'm a paranoid motherfucker.

Frankly I've got a right to be. But unlike some of the other jackasses crawling through the swamp, I don't let it get the better of me. I help Caleb haul the boat into the deeper water. The rumble of the motor sends the swamp into a frenzy around us.

Frogs panic and leap out of our way.

I'm still alive back at the parking lot.

Connor tells us all the story of how Noah shot two ducks and the rest of us fuckers shot none while we haul the hunting gear out of the boat and stow it in the back of the Jeep. Caleb bends down to shove the boat under a nearby shelter.

I feel a thousand times better when the rifles are stowed, too.

Noah and I climb into the back. Caleb takes

his spot behind the wheel. My entire body prepares for the Jeep to swing to the right. It's a shitty, gravel on-ramp and somebody's going to die there someday, but it's not going to be me.

Caleb turns left.

My stomach drops into my feet. He's going the wrong fucking way.

"Did you forget where the city is, mother-fucker?" I keep my voice light. A joke between buddies.

Connor swings around in his seat, his grin apocalyptic. "Should I tell them, boss?"

I catch Caleb's eyes crinkling in the light from the dashboard. His mouth stretches in a hellish smile. "It's going down tonight. First mission."

Fuck. *Fuck.* How the hell can I get myself out of this? One of Caleb's missions is not the plan. The plan is to go back to the city, report to my superiors, and throw some pebbles at Bethany's window. Connor's seat jerks backward under my palm. It settles with a sharp crack—must've been halfway between positions on its rails. "What the fuck, man?" He looks me in the eye. "You scared?"

"Fuck no." I'm not scared. I'm fucking pissed. Pissed that I agreed to this in the first place. Pissed that I was stupid enough not to recognize the signs. Pissed that there's nothing I can say to get Caleb to turn the Jeep around. I know it in my gut. *Goddamn* it.

I watch twenty minutes crawl by on the dashboard clock. It feels like the end of the fucking world. Then Caleb makes a sharp right onto a dirt road. If there was any cover—any cover at all—I'd bail out the side of the Jeep right now. But there's nothing. It's an empty field, the grass cut short. A warehouse looms out of the darkness. A floodlight comes on. I raise a hand on instinct. It's fucking blinding. My eyes lag in adjusting like they want me to die. It can't get any worse than a warehouse in the middle of nowhere. A bead of sweat gathers at the base of my neck and slips down my spine.

Caleb brakes hard.

Oh, fuck.

It's worse.

Now I see them. The lust on Connor's face. The crates, piled high. And the men with guns aimed at us.

CHAPTER SIXTEEN

Katherine Dunham was an African American dancer and anthropologist. In 1931, when she was only twenty-one years old, she formed a group called Ballet Nègres, one of the first black ballet companies in the United States.

BETHANY, FIVE YEARS AGO

THE MINUTES TICK by. I've stretched so much there's a perpetual ache in my hamstrings. It's forty-five minutes past the time he usually comes. *He isn't coming.* I shouldn't have gotten my hopes up. Just because he comes to see me five nights in a row—we aren't boyfriend and girlfriend. We aren't going steady. The fact that I felt that way…that's my fault. A knot in my stomach pulls tighter and tighter. Nervous energy moves me around the room, until finally I have to skip down the stairs just to distract myself from the window.

On the back porch I do a series of slow pirouettes. As slow as I can stand it. Testing my balance. Staying upright. And, yes, picturing how it will look through the window when he sees me. If he sees me. We've never had a formal conversation about any of this. There's no spoken agreement that Joshua North will keep coming to my house every night. I've known all along that this could end at any time. I just never really believed that it would end.

Maybe I still don't.

Ten more pirouettes, the last one so agonizingly slow that my calf starts to cramp. I let my arms fall to my sides. My eyes are perfectly adjusted to the dark. Every time I've faced the back windows, I used the time to scan the yard. There are no solid shadows blotting out the night. None. I find myself in first position. Like I might lift my heel off the floor and let my weight carry me into a spin. Wouldn't that be ironic? *You turn and turn and turn.* That's what he said that day in the cemetery, and that's what I'm doing now.

Time to do something different.

"Bethany?"

Mamere's voice has a worried edge. I whirl around, rising on tiptoe, hand flying to my throat. "Mamere, I didn't know you were still up. Did I wake you?"

"What are you doing out there?" She beckons me close with one hand. "Your bed was empty. I came to find you."

A wave of residual fear and guilt sloshes through my belly. The one night I'm home, she comes looking. If this had been another night, with me down in that basement club that doesn't check IDs, pressed up against Joshua North...a shiver goes through me. She would've woken the neighborhood. A flare of anger burns away the guilt. This is what comes of getting involved with men like that. I never should've trusted him, not for anything. I walk with Mamere back up the stairs. "I couldn't sleep. I needed to move, and I didn't want the noise to wake you up." I give a rueful laugh. "I guess it did anyway."

She puts her hands on either side of my face and pulls my head down to kiss my forehead. "Whatever's troubling you, it'll look better in daylight. Sleep, child. Don't fight your demons in the dark."

Back on my bed I sink into the mattress. There are no more demons to dance with now. Josh isn't coming tonight. We're not together, so he had no obligation to stop by. He had no obligation to tell me that he wouldn't be coming. None whatsoever. But if he believed in common courtesy, he'd have done it anyway. Josh obviously doesn't believe in common courtesy. But he did come here every night for five nights in a row. What's different about tonight? My thoughts go around and around in circles.

You know. You know exactly why he didn't come. The awful, terrible truth of it circles my other errant thoughts. Because he wanted to see if you'd put out for him. That's all anybody's interested in. Your legs spread for a man or for an audience. On a bed or in the air. They all only want one thing.

I want this not to be true for Josh. The things we've done haven't involved beds or even nudity. Only the hot press of his mouth and the expert graze of his fingers. I keep coming back to the same conclusion. That's what he wanted. My mouth. My touch. That's it.

Sleep drifts close, only to tease me and run away again. Over and over and over. I refuse to look at the clock on my bedside table. I don't want to know how much of the night he's stealing from me. At some point I squeeze my eyes closed and resolve to listen to Mamere. *Don't fight your demons in the dark.* I'm trying not to do it, but damn. They won't leave me in peace tonight. He won't leave me in peace. And he's not even here.

Done. I'm done. I'm leaving it behind me. It was a momentary lapse of judgment. That's it. It won't come with me to the future. He won't—

The pebble on my windowpane is like a boulder crashing through water. My thoughts scatter like frightened guppies. My heart pounds. I throw back the blankets and leap to the window. A silent prayer—*let it not be a branch, or a bird, or anything else*—

It's him.

In my scramble to climb out the window I don't get a good look at him. As soon as my feet hit the ground I'm turning, words tumbling from my lips. "Where were you? I thought you'd be— what happened?"

"What do you mean?" His voice is harsh, mocking. "What makes you think anything happened, sweetheart?" His hands are buried in his pockets. The cocky stance only highlights the dark stain on his shirt. The stain is almost as dark as the expression he wears. It's made worse by the hard relief of the moonlight. The shadows cut across his face, splitting his sneer in two. "And here I thought I looked handsome."

"You have blood on your shirt." There's not enough oxygen to say anything else, though I probably sound ridiculous. There's probably some perfectly reasonable explanation. *I was walking on the sidewalk and tripped.* "Where were you?"

"At a party," he spits. "A gathering of some close friends. It was a celebration. Can't you tell?"

He's so big, so solid, and so angry that it makes me want to shrink away. But I'm not going to shrink from this. Not a chance in hell. My heartbeat is louder than any of the familiar night sounds. It blocks them all out until I feel like I'm standing on the inside of a bass drum. I swallow an acid fear. I take a step closer. "How did you get the blood on your shirt, Josh? Who did this to you?"

He looks away with a huffed breath. I brace for another mean response. Shock comes off him in waves. I've felt it coming off my brother before. I've felt it gathering on my own skin. At that time I was only six. I didn't know what it meant, only that it felt like all the world was collapsing in on me. Caleb was the only one holding its crushing weight at bay. *You weren't here.* The urgent whisper crawls up from the darkest corner of my memory. *You were in your bed, sleeping. When we woke up in the morning, we found him like this. Go to sleep. Go back to sleep. We weren't here.*

Josh turns back to me slowly, like he's not quite sure I'll still be standing in front of him when our eyes meet. I don't move. His cheek twitches. A line of blood divides the skin there, too. "It was Caleb."

No. "He did this to you?" My lungs cave in. "Why? Did you have a fight?"

"Did we have a fight," he whispers under his breath. "You were lying to me before. You had to have been."

"Lying about what? I wasn't lying about anything." My palms start to sweat. "What are you talking about?"

He forces his fingers through his hair. "You acted like you didn't know anything. How could you not have known about this?"

"Whoa." This is so horribly unfair. "Hang on. I don't know what you're talking about. Tell me what you're talking about."

"He's in deep." Josh's voice drops to a deadly softness. "Deep in some shady business. And I'm not talking about a local drug ring. I'm not talking about small-time black-market bullshit. It's way bigger than that." He's studying me like I might give something away. I have nothing to show him except a creeping sense of dread.

"I knew he was…I knew he sold things. Guns." My voice trembles. Why? Why can't I sound strong and sure in this moment? "Weapons. But—" What possible defense is there for what my brother does? I know it skirts some laws. "No. He sells guns to people who want them. That's all."

"Well, when you say it like that, it sounds perfectly reasonable. Jesus, Bethany." Josh's expression darkens into incredulous hatred. "He's not selling guns to gang members. It's worse than that by orders of magnitude. Are you really this naive?"

"I'm not naive," I shoot back. "I know he's not a good person, okay? I know that. But I don't believe—what could be worse?" I throw my hands up. Try to get a handle on my voice. "What could be worse than what he already does? Maybe you're the one who's naive." It's a losing argument and I know it. I just can't stop. "What could be worse than what he already does?" The question comes out plaintive and small.

"He sells weapons, Bethany. But he's not selling them to homegrown killers, which is already a fucked-up thing to do, if you ask me." Josh's voice has gone absolutely even. Almost casual. He tilts his face to the moon. It was better when he was angry. A million times better. "He sells them to foreign operatives."

"F-foreign operatives?" My brother has always

flirted with the wrong side of the law, ever since our father died. I knew the army was a means to an end. I knew he'd find a way to twist it for his own purposes. "I'm sorry, I—How is that so much worse?"

Josh nods, understanding dawning on his face. The understanding that I really am this stupid. *I'm not stupid*, I want to scream at him. *You have blood on your shirt and my brother is to blame.* "How do I make this clear?" he muses at the moon. Then he looks me dead in the eye. "He sells to enemy governments. Terrorists. People who dedicate their entire existence to killing Americans by any means necessary. Do you know what that is, Bethany?"

My name on his lips in this context freezes me where I stand. Because I *do* know. On some level I know what Josh is about to say. I paid attention in US history class. I made As on every test. This isn't that hard to figure out, but I don't want to know the answer.

"It's treason."

I can't breathe.

Josh shrugs. There's only a hint of defeat in the movement. I don't think he regrets this at all. "I'm turning him in."

"No," I gasp.

"I have no other choice."

We learned about this in school. The United States government executes people for treason. They could do the same to my brother. If Josh is telling the truth, they could take Caleb to federal prison and release him in a coffin. Horror engulfs me, surrounding me as surely as the moonlight. My brother is a dangerous man. He associates with other dangerous men. He does dangerous things. But when I was a little girl, he put his body between me and the man who came at me with harm in his fists. That connection can't be broken, even by treason. I have a duty to him. Even now. I owe Caleb my life. I have to try to spare his. It takes me two tries to speak. "You do have another choice. You do."

Now Josh's expression softens. He looks almost sorry for me. "I can't let him put American weapons in the hands of our enemies." He looks away, and his face in profile is among the most beautiful sights I've ever seen. "I'm no hero. But I can't let it get that far. I think you know that."

I seize the tiny, thin thread of hope. "I do know that." Desperation chokes me, both hands around my neck. "Of course you can't let him do what he's planning to do." For all I know, he's already done it. For all I know, Josh is stopping a machine that's already in progress. "But is there any way—" Emotion cuts my voice off at the knees. It's nothing but a whisper now. "Is there any way you could help him live? Please."

JOSH, FIVE YEARS AGO

BETHANY LOOKS AT me, eyes brimming with tears for her scumbag of a brother. The man who puts deadly weapons in the hands of people who want to watch Americans die for the sheer pleasure of it. Caleb wants money more than he wants to protect our brothers-in-arms. He wants money more than he wants to keep innocent people on both sides of the ocean safe. I should hate her, too.

But all I can see is how achingly beautiful she is.

Caleb's little sister tilts her face up toward mine, leaving nothing to the imagination. All her hope and fear is laid bare. She doesn't shy away from what she's asking. And even then, the words pale in comparison to the full sweep of her lips. The slight tremble there makes me want to press my thumb against that flesh and worship there forever.

It's truly fucked.

The pain is like nothing I've ever felt. Ringing through every cell like a wet rag twisted in violent hands. Bleeding it dry until there's no moisture left. Nothing to make a heart beat. She's kryptonite. She's killing me.

I would do anything for her.

It hits like a sucker punch. All my life I've been dodging fists. I thought I was past the days of being taken by surprise. But this? This is true shock. Down to the bone. Down to the marrow.

Anything. Anything at all. I'd sell out my country for her. I have to bite the tip of my tongue from telling her that of course I'll spare her brother. Of course I'll let him live. I'll let him keep up with his horrendous fuckery no matter how many people die. The blood on my hands won't matter at all, if I can only give her what she wants.

Bethany is hope embodied. Her weight shifts in the wind. She could take flight at any moment. I know exactly where she would go—directly into my arms. She'd breathe her thank-you into my ear, her arms locked tight around my neck. I would press her body to mine. It would be a tremendous relief, to have her that close. Jesus, I need it. I need it like I need to breathe. I need it like I need my heart to beat.

I need it too fucking much.

That's the endgame.

I can't be that vulnerable. Not for Bethany. Not for anyone. Not for the rest of my life. I lean in close enough that I can see the look in her eyes. If I'm going to do this, I'm going to bear witness to every part of it. I'm not going to look away. "No."

Her lips curve upward in a smile that's incandescent with relief before she registers what I've said. Then it all comes crashing down. Her eyes fly open wide, wider than I thought possible. The knife twists in my gut, scraping my organs.

"What?" She's horrified. Shaking.

"No, I won't help you." The laugh that tears from my throat is the cruelest sound I've ever heard, and I spent years living with my father. I'm dying. If I can stay upright, it'll be a fucking miracle. "Is there any way I can help him? Unfucking-believable. I always knew Caleb was a goddamn fool. I thought you were smarter than that."

Bethany takes a half step back, eyes flying around the yard like she's searching for a hidden camera. "But you—you took me out. You came to see me—why did you do that?" Her voice is high and thin, like she can't get a full breath.

Neither can I.

"You have a killer body, sweetheart. I wanted to fuck you. That's it."

And I'll be damned, damned for all eternity, because fresh hope lights her eyes. She steps back into the ring. "If you do, then maybe—"

"Fuck, Bethany." I grab for her, hooking one hand around the back of her neck and yanking her in close. This is my one concession. I'm going to take this one thing like the selfish fucking bastard that I am. I can feel her hope and hesitation through the palm of my hand. I'm cutting her as deep as I know how, and she's still holding out hope. Lowering my mouth to her ear, I take one last breath of her. "Do you honestly think your pussy is worth that much?"

Bethany's shoulders sag, a half-sob escaping her, and she pulls herself back. Her hands go to her stomach, and she presses in on some invisible stab wound. "Stop." There's almost no voice behind the word, only breath. "Don't say that."

"But it's true." I taunt her even though the words scorch my throat. "Little Bethany Lewis thinks her precious pussy is worth committing treason for. That I'd give up turning in one of the nation's worst criminals for a mediocre fuck. As if I even wanted that." She shakes her head wordlessly. No, no, no. "Yes. You're not even worth a fuck to me." I shiver like the thought disgusts me. "Your body is nothing special. You can turn in your music box all you want, but you'll never be anything more than the sister of a criminal. A poor little wretch, clawing for scraps. That's you, Bethany. That will always be you. And there's not a fucking thing you can do about it."

I can't believe I'm still drawing air into my lungs. I can't believe the universe hasn't struck me down. I can't believe I'm still standing.

Bethany swallows hard. The moon shines brighter than a floodlight, so I get a front-row seat to every moment of the pain I'm causing her. Her fists shake against her belly. For a terrible moment I think she might really have a knife sprouting from her skin. I would believe it if my barbed words had become barbed metal.

It's fucking unbearable. This is it. This is the thing that breaks me. That shatters my spine and leaves me broken at her feet. I've survived all this time only to tear myself apart in the name of some fucked-up need to remain invulnerable.

Bethany straightens up.

It's slow and painful. It's all I can do not to reach out to her.

Even in her agony, she can't shed her inherent grace. When she's at her full height, she looks up at me. It doesn't matter that I'm bigger and stronger and mean to the core. The look she levels me with is beyond all of that. It's the look of a queen passing final judgment on behalf of her realm. The wind goes silent around us. The babble of the creek in its low bed ceases. Everything on the earth bows before her.

Everything except me.

She doesn't seem to notice that I'm the heretic. I'm as much under her command as the clouds above us and the grass below. So it feels worse than exile when she pronounces my sentence.

One word, and one word only. She delivers it looking deeply into my eyes. Bethany lets her silvery tears run free down her cheeks, but her jaw doesn't shake, and her voice is clear. The penalty for what I've done is nonnegotiable. There is no room for interpretation. No going back.

"Leave."

CHAPTER SEVENTEEN

The dancing plague of 1518 was a case of dancing mania that occurred in modern day France. Around four hundred people, mostly female, danced for days without rest, some of whom died from heart attack, stroke and exhaustion. Modern theories for the mania include food poisoning or stress-induced psychosis.

BETHANY, FIVE YEARS AGO

THE SWING CREAKS underneath me while I sway back and forth in the dark. The rusty chains dig into my palms. This thing is a death trap. I could get tetanus or something. But it probably doesn't matter, because I already feel dead.

Dead for days. Dead for the rest of my life. Dead, dead, dead.

Or at least empty, which is as good as dead. Time doesn't care. It's hurtling forward without any regard for the fact that my world spun off its axis.

Josh left days ago. A lifetime ago.

So did my brother.

They were here, and then they were gone.

The family liaison at the army base won't tell me a goddamn thing. They confirm that Caleb is still on leave, like it's some kind of script. How can they lie like that? That's what I want to know. How can they take my calls and feed me some line about record keeping and checkpoints when they have to know?

Overgrown weeds tickle the tops of my feet. I used to be afraid of weeds like this growing up. I thought something might be lurking in there that would reach up and grab me. Now I know better than to waste my emotions on weeds. The real terrors in the world are up here in broad daylight, bringing you beignets. I take a deep breath of the night air. I'm going to have to head in soon, though being in the house makes me feel like a bird trapped in a cage. I have to be more careful, now that Caleb's gone. Mamere is more sensitive to when I'm gone. I don't want her to worry.

Well, maybe she doesn't have to worry now.

The worst thing has already come through our yard with a fistful of pebbles to throw at my window. It's turned in my brother to the US

Army and sent him packing down the road to his death. I know Josh did his duty. That's the one thing I have no doubt about. He did the right thing, even if it killed me. No matter how hard I try, I can't scrub his face that night from my mind. Or his words.

"I tried," I whisper down into the weeds.

Lightning bugs wheel lazily through the grass, tracing a haphazard path to the oak tree. They disappear behind the Spanish moss and reappear moments later. In and out of sight. Sooner or later they'll be gone for good.

Like everything else in my life.

Everything is in ruins. I'm Pompeii. Another place we learned about in history class. They couldn't save themselves, either. A layer of ash that suffocated them.

"Bethany."

I must have imagined the low voice behind me.

I only turn my head to prove myself right. And then my heart tumbles out of my chest and falls with a muffled thud to the ground. The swing sticks to my legs, molten rubber. I tear myself away from it in a flash of pain. My bare feet land in the tall, scratchy grass. Three hard blinks and he's still there. "Caleb."

He stands in the center of the yard.

Twenty feet from here, in the kitchen, he protected me from our father at the height of his anger and drunkenness. In this light, in this place, it's shocking how much Caleb looks like him. My stomach does a sick turn.

My brother has become the man he fought and killed as a child. How could I have missed it? My heartbeat sounds a warning. It's not relief I feel after all. It's fear. I have always known that Caleb was dangerous in the abstract.

Now it couldn't be more real.

I want to back away. The urge makes my feet ache, but I can't show him any weakness. I know it at the most base level. "I thought you were in trouble," I blurt out, saying anything to break the silence. "Josh told me—" *Shit.* "I—"

Caleb shifts his weight, making himself look bigger. He's still several feet away, but he manages to loom over me. He looks so much like our father that I feel faint. "You have a crush on him?" he growls, mouth twisting.

I suppress the urge to run. "No. Of course not." I shake my head a little, like this is the most absurd thing I've ever heard. Well, that part's true enough. What I feel for Josh can't be described using a word like *crush*. It's more like an obsession.

"That fucker rolled over on me. Almost." He looks up at the stars. There's no moon to illuminate his face tonight, only the ambient light from the city around us. "He ratted out my shipment. Cost me a lot of money, but I'm not rotting in a jail cell." Caleb spits into the grass. "I suppose that's reason enough for me not to kill him."

If my brother knew how Josh had touched me, he would want to kill him. And he'd do it. That much I know. Caleb isn't much for holding back.

"Fucker," Caleb says. "How are you doing? Anybody mess with you while I was gone?"

Nobody did, but I can't gather the words to speak. *I'm not rotting in a jail cell.* Caleb is standing here, in the backyard of Mamere's house. Which means that Josh did what I asked, even though he said he wouldn't. My heart squeezes.

"No," I manage. "Nobody messed with me."

But someone *did* save my brother. The gratitude that flows from my broken heart is potent enough to drown me. It's laced with a regret so strong it brings tears to my eyes. Was it wrong to ask Josh to save him?

Should I have wanted him to be spared?

I don't know whether my loyalty lies with my father or with Caleb—or whether they're even that different, in the end. I don't know whether I owe more to my brother or to a stranger with green eyes. What does loyalty mean in a world of betrayal?

"Good." Caleb checks his watch. "I've got business. You keep your eyes open." He disappears around the side of the house before I have a chance to answer. My murderous traitor of a brother. He's safe now—because of me.

I dig my knuckles into my chest hard enough to leave a mark. What have I done? What have I done? The look on Josh's face when I begged for Caleb's life told me that the true scope of his crimes was unforgivable.

Beyond redemption.

If my brother is beyond redemption, then maybe I am, too.

CHAPTER EIGHTEEN

Martha Graham created and choreographed one of her most famous works, Heretic, in one night. One of her students remembered the creation this way: "It was a pleading figure against a hostile group—terse, brief, stark; I think no other dance quite represented her personal statement with such power."

JOSH, PRESENT TIME

THERE ARE TWO faces on my computer monitor. Liam is older than me, only by a year. He has green eyes, exactly like our father. Elijah is three years younger than me, but the shadows haunting his dark green eyes make him look wiser than both of the other North brothers. Elijah's filling us in on his latest mission in Colombia, where an extraction has gone smoothly—baring a few fatalities from the cartel.

"Good work," Liam says, his expression stoic. "The general has been on my ass about this Russia deal, and we need you back in the mix."

Liam founded the company on his network in the security business and ironclad reputation. He's the one in charge of managing the CEOs, the military brass, the celebutantes who hire the company. I'm the operations man. I keep tabs on which team goes where. I'm in charge of hiring and training. At least I was… until two weeks ago, when I walked off our base in the Hill Country of Texas to fly to Louisiana.

"Copy that," Elijah says, ignoring the fact that he hasn't had a day off in about three years running. He prefers action, the more dangerous the better. He's basically been on a suicide mission since he left the army. His green eyes meet mine. "Unless you need any help with that dancer."

Liam doesn't move a muscle, but I feel his curiosity in the pixels. I never told my brothers about my history with Bethany, but they aren't fucking stupid. They know I've kept a house in New Orleans. Not hard to speculate it's because of a woman.

"It's under control," I say, my voice light.

"Is it?" Liam presses a few keys on his computer. "I'm looking at these reports you got from intel. Weapons smuggling. Human trafficking. Drug running. This guy isn't playing around. I'm not sure a two man team is enough."

"He's probably not the perp."

"Caleb Lewis?"

"No one."

Quiet over the line. Both men regard me with similar expressions of subtle disbelief. There's no way I'm fooling them, but I'm not about to open up my emotions, either. We had that shit beat out of us early. "You ever wonder what would've happened if we'd gotten together and killed that motherfucker?"

Neither of them have to ask who I'm talking about. There's only one motherfucker we would have wanted to kill. Our father lived to terrorize us until the very last of us left. He was strong and merciless, but there were three of us. Even scrawny and half-starved we could've killed him— the way Caleb did his father.

Liam looks away from the camera. A muscle moves in his jaw. "Been thinking about him lately. You know that shit runs in families? Like green eyes or brown hair. Genetics or some shit. They've done papers on it."

"You're not gonna be like him," Elijah says, his voice low and fierce.

I snort. "Samantha would probably kill you if you were."

We all go quiet at that, remembering a mother who stood up for us only to get beaten back down. It happened one too many times.

One day, she wasn't there anymore. Liam and I got home from school, and Elijah was in the house, only three years old, sitting at the kitchen table. Alone. I walked into the house two seconds before Liam, and I'll never forget the way those wide green eyes blinked up at me. He wasn't crying. Even then, he knew no one would be there to answer him. We never saw her after that day. Further proof that Liam will make an amazing father. He took care of me and Elijah until the day he enlisted.

Liam runs a hand over his face. "She has us seeing some shrink who says a lot of new age shit about manifesting our future, but I don't know what wishful thinking has ever done. There's only guns and knives, and neither of those help with a diaper."

"There's violins," I say, because my brother looks seriously distraught. "We all choose our weapons. And yeah, none of that shit is gonna help with a diaper. You're gonna figure that out on your own, and you'll do great, and when you don't do great, you'll pass off the little runt to Uncle Joshua."

Liam grunts. "No way you're coming near him."

"Is it a boy?" Elijah asks.

"Nah, we don't know yet. I'm just trying to manifest it, because what the hell would I know about a girl?"

"You literally raised one," I say, not even trying to hide my amusement. He got custody of Samantha Brooks, the prodigy violinist, when she was only twelve years old. Not a baby, sure, but he bought plenty of pink shit.

He frowns at me, because he still has guilt about fucking her when she was all grown up. Good thing Samantha has them going to that shrink. "If the new age shit doesn't work I'll just pummel some sense into you."

"Get in line," Elijah says, because he grew up bigger and meaner than both of us. He really could pound us into the concrete. Not that he'd need to. Liam took care of me and Elijah and Samantha. He'll carry the whole fucking world on his shoulders. Of course he'll take care of this little infant. The bigger question is whether he'll give himself even a moment to actually enjoy the experience. Probably not.

The door to my office opens, and I swing around.

Noah's holding a manila envelope like it's an IED primed to go off.

"I'm out," I say to the mic before clicking off the call. The expression Noah wears makes my heart pound. Liam can wait. He'll probably call me back in thirty seconds, pissed that I cut him off, but I don't care. "What is it?"

He steps closer and hands the folder over. "The results from the analysis lab."

I have the envelope torn open before he finishes the sentence. The fucking flower. If we're going to find the bastard, we need to know where the flower came from. It's much harder to trace paper these days, with copy shops on every corner. You can have a document printed from anywhere in the world, to any UPS store, and all that's left is a cold digital trail.

The information I need is right there. Black-and-white. "They found it."

Noah leans in. "Where?"

"Edge of the Garden District." The name of the shop isn't as important as the interview. I've used this private investigator before, and she does her due diligence. It's why I'm willing to pay her high fees. She identified the type of tulip and interviewed florist shops until she found the right one.

I flip through the pages and drink in the transcript from the phone call. "'I remember this guy,'" I read aloud. "'He had a scar in his hair. Dark hair, but the scar I remember.'" Noah and I lock eyes over the desk. There's only one person I know with a scar running through his hair in a way distinctive enough for the owner of a flower shop to mention it twice. Coincidence? Not fucking likely. "Connor."

Fuck. The past is coming back to haunt her. To haunt us.

Noah folds his hands in front of him. He looks pissed off. A scary motherfucker. That's why I like him in my goddamn corner. "Want me to tell her?"

"No." This is my responsibility. It's been my responsibility from the first day I saw Bethany dancing in that warehouse. No matter what happens, even if she's an ocean away, her safety will always be my responsibility. "I'll go."

I know where I'll find her at this time of day. Dancing, of course.

She uses my personal gym, which is on the second floor of the house. It was actually a ballroom when I bought the place, as if I might host a goddamn soiree. I laid down mats wall to wall and moved in my weights, my treadmill, my equipment.

When Bethany moved in, I had one side of the large, airy space cleared out so she could have room to stretch her legs. The old ballroom floor is actually perfect for dance. It keeps her from visiting the theater late at night to practice, so it's purely a practical move. I tell myself it has nothing to do with imagining her staying here long after the threat is gone.

Bethany has music playing from the overhead speakers, filling the space while she moves. Only half the lights shine onto the glossy mats. The shadows she casts are a sensual partner to her jumps and twirls. Mirrors on the wall reflect her beautiful body. She looks...free. And what I'm about to tell her will change that. It will cage her. Fear makes bars stronger than iron or steel. That's the real reason why we never got together and killed our father. Because we were afraid of what would happen if we failed. Afraid of what would happen if we succeeded. That's one thing Caleb has never had—fear. The same thing that made him a traitor allowed him to protect his sister.

Fuck, I hate this. There's no good way to break this news. It's one thing to be stalked by a crazy stranger. Another to be stalked by someone you know. Connor isn't likely to be deterred by anything short of superior firepower. Maybe not even that.

A burst of music. She sinks to the floor into a split, then spins on the floor, bouncing right up again, thrusting her fists into the air. This is a new routine she's practicing. It looks like she nailed it.

The song plays its final melancholy notes. Silence.

Only then do I step over the threshold. It seems better than cutting her off in the middle of the song. Her eyes are closed. She looks blissed out by the movement, and I hate that there's a reason for her to be afraid. *Don't fucking ruin it.* I can leave as quietly as I came, and she'll never know I was here.

"Josh?"

So much for that. "I don't want to interrupt you."

"I'm done." She's glowing, a smile on her face, brown skin glistening. "That was my final run-through for the night. I got it. It's in my bones now." She holds her wrists out in front of her and twists them, first one way, then the other. "What did you think?"

You look goddamn magnificent. "Looks different than what you do in the theater."

She shrugs. "That's Landon's stuff. Not

mine."

"Why don't you do that stuff onstage?"

A smile flickers across her full lips. "Maybe. Someday. For now it's enough to dance when I'm alone. And maybe for you to watch, too."

This breaks my heart—this version of Bethany. I recognize it for what it is. The version of her that exists in relative safety. A safety I'm about to crush under my heel. "We got information about that flower."

Her smile fades. A light dims. "What about it?"

I cross the gym with quick strides, my footsteps echoing against the pristine white walls. This is my only time for rehearsal, and I still don't have the perfect lines straight by the time I reach her. I dive in anyway. What else can I do? "The lab was able to trace the flower from your locker to a shop in the Garden District."

She laughs, a joyless sound. "Of course it's from the Garden District." She can't follow through with the joke, can't pretend to be casual about this. Her breath catches on a sob she won't let me see. "Was that it, then? A dead end?"

"No, we got more. The owner was able to give a description of the buyer." Dread makes me hesitate, but only for an instant. "We don't have a positive ID, but based on the physical description—it sounds like Connor."

Her face falls, and she takes in three rapid breaths and turns away from me. Bethany, ever the dancer, angles herself so that her face is partially obscured from the mirrors on the opposite wall. Her whole life is built on a performance. I want the Bethany who's backstage. I want the one she doesn't show other people, but right now I only have the stage. She's projecting an image; it's all I deserve.

This is where I should leave it. She has all the information I have to give. I should go. *Leave her the fuck alone.*

That stubborn humanity at the center of me, the one I've tried to stamp out again and again, forces its way to the front of my mind. I tried to make myself less than human. A robot. A killing machine. It didn't work. I'm still a man. And I still want to comfort her. Without sex. Without all the entanglements that would squeeze the air from our lives. I just need a gesture. Something that will let me hold back.

I need to hold back for both our sakes.

The air in the studio sings with my own anticipation, a crescendo of my own making. It's a goddamn stampede, crashing louder and louder. I take the last step forward. We're almost touching—almost, almost—and then we are. I fold my arms around Bethany from behind, gathering her to my chest.

She melts against me instantly, her head falling back to my shoulder. Jesus, I want her. The scent of her hair is intoxicating. I'll never get over it. I'll never breathe enough of her. This body of mine, it's weak. I have to master the desire. I have to ignore the deep cravings surging through my blood. It multiplies with every second until there's too much to contain. Breathe it out. I have to breathe it out. This is about Bethany, not about what my body wants from hers. *Stop being such a fucking asshole.*

Bethany turns in my arms.

For a moment I see her at age sixteen, moonlight glinting off the tears on her cheeks. A single blink clears my vision. It's still her face. It's still heartbreakingly beautiful. Her heart is still there in her eyes, even after all these years. It's there for me. How have I ever resisted her? There's no one but her.

And I'm lost. I'm utterly fucking lost.

CHAPTER NINETEEN

Break dancing originated in New York City during the late 1960s and early 1970s from martial arts moves developed by street gangs. The moves, originally learned as a form of self-defense against other gangs, eventually evolved into the stylized moves that emphasize energy, creativity, and an element of danger.

BETHANY, PRESENT TIME

W HEN I DANCE someone else's steps, I'm giving my body to their vision.

It's a powerful experience. Joyful and exhilarating, but it doesn't compare to dancing my own dreams. Maybe if Josh had come to me when I was practicing the steps for Landon's new idea, this wouldn't have happened.

Maybe if I still worried about Josh using me for my body, I could resist him.

I'm standing here in a leotard and tights, but my heart is completely naked. It's been stripped bare by dance and by fear. There are no walls with which to guard me. As I look into Josh's green eyes, I'm not sure why I ever wanted those walls.

Dance doesn't only happen in one direction. It's a give-and-take. A two-way street. Something that I perform. Something that he receives. In this moment his heart is in his emerald eyes. He's been stripped bare by the dance and the fear, too.

"Josh," I whisper.

He shakes his head as if breaking a trance. "You don't want to do this."

That makes me smile. "How do you know?"

"I know." He doesn't smile back.

His gaze is hard and dark. What I see there makes me shiver. He wants me. Was that ever a question? He's always wanted my body. A lot of men watch me that way. There's something else. A raw need that it doesn't seem like one person could soothe.

"Because I'll expect too much?" I ask, facing him head on. "Because I'll think you love me. Because I'll think I love you. Because I'll expect a happily ever after?"

"Because I'll hurt you." His voice is flat, without any hint of smugness.

Without any apology.

What would it be like to go through life believing you were a weapon, incapable of doing anything but hurting the people who get close? There's a certain kind of hollowness, knowing that men only want to use my body for pleasure.

What would it be like to believe you can only cause pain?

I'll never convince him otherwise. I'm not even sure he's wrong. Whatever's happening between us—it will break my heart. It's already breaking. I lift his hand, shocked at how even this part of him is heavy with muscle. I press his palm flat against my chest, in the place between my breasts. Standing far away, he could be an ordinary-sized man. Like this, it's clear how large he is. How powerful. His thumb rests against one breast. His pinky finger against the other. My heart beats erratically beneath the weight. "Then hurt me."

He stares at me, the conflict plain in his gaze. There are a thousand battles fought in the span of seconds. I should probably give him time to consider the consequences. Instead I lick my lips. It isn't something conscious. It's as if my body is preparing itself for sex, as if it knows what this will feel like even if my mind does not. *An ambush.* The war is over.

He lifts his hand to my mouth, tracking the

path of my tongue. It's wet and crude and somehow sweet at the same time. Scars on his fingertips drag along my lips, the way mountains jut into the sky. He's the jagged line; I'm the endless blue.

"I'm going to kiss you here," he says, his voice almost conversational. He could be giving me instructions for our security detail. This could be routine. "I'm going to fuck you here, too. There's no part of this body I won't touch and bend and use. Understand?"

Wrong. He shouldn't be talking to me this way, and I definitely shouldn't like it. My whole life I've been fighting against the idea that men can use my body. I've been kicking and screaming against society's demands—only to discover they turn me on. Well, not any man. Not every man. Joshua North. When he says those words, they turn me on.

"What if I say no?" The question comes out coy, and I'm not even sure how I want him to answer—as the man who's protecting me or as the asshole I've always wanted.

"Then I stop." The corner of his mouth turns up. It's a smile without humor, without doubt. "You aren't going to want me to stop. Not until I'm through with you."

A clench between my legs. "You're pretty confident."

"I fuck the way I do everything else. Mean. You come when I say so." Heavy lids hood those green eyes, making him look sinister, underscoring his words. "We stop, you don't get to come."

I should want someone like Landon, someone who has the same interests as me, someone who understands the life of a dancer. I should like any one of the men who come to my performances, who look at me like I'm a figurine in a music box. They would never talk to me this way. And I would never feel this pulsing, aching sense of being alive.

"Prove it," I say, lifting my chin away from his touch.

Half of me braces for impact, as if he might rip the leotard off my body, as if he might slam me into the mats. He has more patience than I gave him credit for. More strategy.

He smiles. "Say no, Bethany."

He traces the line of my cheek with his forefinger. Sensation suffuses my body. His finger is a heat source, and my body is pure metal. I'm conducting everything he gives me. There's complete concentration as he draws his finger down to my jaw—and lower, lower, to the tendon in my neck. He takes his time. So much time, as if this is the only thing he ever wanted to do to me, as if his finger pad on my pulse point is the culmination of our entire sexual encounter.

I understand now why I'd never say no— because I'm desperate for more. "Yes," I whisper.

The back of his hand brushes over my breast, back and forth, back and forth, until my nipple hardens, until it shoves against the fabric, small and sharp. He squeezes the tip, making me moan. Harder. Harder. Hard enough that I let out a squeak of protest. Then he does let me go, and the feeling is enough to make me light-headed. It doesn't feel good, exactly. This isn't chocolate milk. It's a shot of whiskey that burns down my throat and warms low in my belly.

"Should I?" I tug at the shoulder strap of my leotard, ready to take it off. The stretchy fabric has held me like a second skin through hours of practice and performance—suddenly it feels like it's made of horsehair. Scratchy. Tight. I want it off my body, so he can touch me, the real me.

A flick of his fingers. Sharp pain on the back of my hand. "No," he says. "I want you to wear it. I want you to keep it on so you always remember this. No matter where you go, you'll always remember how it felt to be full of me, to be on your knees with my cock in your mouth and my fingers in your cunt, and when you're onstage in front of a thousand people, the memory will make you wet."

It's making me wet right now. I'm slick between my legs. If he felt the strip of fabric, it would already be damp, and I don't know how I'm going to wear this in front of a thousand people.

He pinches my other nipple, and I shudder against the pain and pleasure. "Say no, Bethany. That's what you want to say. 'Leave me alone. Don't touch me. Keep your filthy hands off my sweet body.'"

A hitch in my breath. "What if you say no?"

Then he does laugh, and the sound has no cynicism. It's almost boyish with its unguarded joy. "I'm not saying no to you, Bethany. I've never said no to you."

He sobers. I do, too, because he's right about that. He never said no to me, even when I asked him to put aside his principles to protect my family. He said yes. "I'm sorry," I whisper because I've never said that to him. Even knowing how this ends, I couldn't have made another choice. I owed my brother my life, but Josh? He didn't owe me anything.

"If you say no, I still get to come. The same way I've come every night since I met you, fucking my fist, imagining your legs spread wide for me, your mouth open as I ride you."

JOSH, PRESENT TIME

I SAID TOO much.

She doesn't need to know how much power she has over me. Bad enough that I've been panting over a woman who's been across the globe for most of these years. The idea struck me as fucking funny. That I would say no to her—to her little tits and her long legs? She could flay my skin open with a hot poker, and I'd be here saying, *Yes, Bethany. Anything you want.* In some ways the hot poker would be easier than this. Her eyes flay me open, liquid brown and full of undeserved trust.

"On your knees," I tell her, keeping my voice hard.

The dilemma's clear on her pretty face. She wants to tell me to go to hell, but she wants to orgasm on my dick even more. *I'm sorry,* I want to tell her. *I'm sorry your biology makes you want stupid fuckers like me. I'm sorry your little vagina wants to be full of hard cock.*

That's not what I actually say, though. "Tick tock."

A flash of defiance. It's chased away by glazed desire. She drops to her knees, and the sight of her there is almost enough to make me come. "Now what?" she asks, her hands twisting in her lap. She's nervous and excited and turned on as fuck, and it's all I can do not to come in my pants. One pull and I'd be jizzing all over her smooth skin and worn leotard.

I make myself open my pants in a slow, deliberate way. It's the anticipation that gets her hot. "If I were a gentleman, I'd put you in a bed and lick your pussy until you creamed on my face. If I were a gentleman, I wouldn't nut until you'd come once, twice, three times." The cold air feels like knives on my cock. I'm so fucking swollen I have to pinch the end of my dick to hold it in. "I'm not a gentleman, am I?"

She doesn't answer me. Or maybe she does answer me, by leaning forward to lick the tip of my cock. I suck in a breath, and God, God, her little tongue. If she had sucked me, I might have been able to withstand the onslaught, might have lost myself in physical sensation. Instead she licked me right on the tip, and it was so goddamn adorable.

"Again," I grunt, pushing my hips toward her.

She licks me again, and I have to grit my teeth against the surge of climax. I hold it back, barely, but there's no more time for her to drive me insane. I flip her over, so she's got no choice but to be on her hands and knees. Beautiful ass up. Cheek pressed to the mat. One upside of fucking a dancer—her body is designed to be moved however I want. She can hold the position for hours. I won't last nearly that long. With two fingers I pull the placket of her leotard aside. Her pussy's shaven smooth, and I have to fight against the urge to lick her. Patience, patience.

Part of me wants to shove my bare dick inside her. I've never fucked a girl raw, and the urge has never been this strong. To feel her secret muscles pulse around me. To come inside her and see the seed dripping out. Christ. Some deeply buried shred of decency forces me to dig in my pocket for a condom. I wrap up and press the head of my cock to her folds.

I brace my hands on her hips, more to steady myself than her. A long, hard thrust finds me inside her body, and I can't contain the groan of satisfaction. That sound doesn't hide the whimper she makes. Her whole body's vibrating like a pulled tendon. Her hands curl into fists against the mats on the floor.

One. Two. Three. I give her the seconds to adjust, but it only seems to get worse. "Bethany," I mutter, fighting with myself for control. "How long has it been?"

Her body is flexible and strong. I never imagined she'd have trouble taking my cock, even if she hadn't been with a man in a while. Her muscles feel like a vise.

I slap her hip to force an answer. "How long?"

A gasp, and for a second I think she might be laughing. Then I realize it's a quiet sob. "I've never—I haven't—I'm sorry."

Oh no. Oh fuck. She's a virgin?

This cunt that's holding me like I've finally found home. A virgin. I drop my forehead to her back. "I'm the one who's sorry, sweet thing. I didn't know. I didn't think. And I can't even pull out and fuck you the right way, because you feel like fucking heaven."

"Don't you dare stop," she says, her tone so fervent that I let out an unsteady laugh.

"Adorable. How can you be so sexy and adorable at the same time?"

In slow degrees I feel her relax her body. It's not something that happens on its own. It's a force of will, because she's an athlete. She can master the pain of an eight-hour workout. She can push through the wall that tells ordinary people to stop. That's how she takes my cock—as a challenge.

"Do it," she says, like a prayer, a chant. "Do it, do it, do it."

I'm caught between her body and the moral thing to do. That's always where I'm caught. It's the space where I've lived my life since I first saw her dance in that shadowed warehouse years ago. I should pull out of her body and walk away. Or at the very least I should come in a degrading spray across her body. Then she'd really learn to hate me. Instead I fuck her in small movements, careful thrusts, forcing myself to be gentle with her—as much as I can with my dick wedged in her clenched channel.

I press a kiss to the back of her neck, and she shivers. I do it again and again and again until I find a place that makes her pussy clamp hard. The climax starts at the base of my spine. It blinds me, until I'm sucking the back of her shoulder, bucking against her like an animal, being milked by the spasms of her pussy as I make her feel nothing but pain.

We collapse in a pile of sweaty limbs. A gentleman would never crush a lady, but I land on her with no grace and no concern for her well-being. She's strong enough to take it. That's the best thing I can say for me—that I picked a woman strong enough to survive the way I fuck.

When I finally manage to pull myself up, she's still sprawled on the mats, her legs bent, chest rising and falling in an endless pant. She looks relieved. She hasn't come yet, but she still looks relieved, because she survived the ordeal that was Joshua North.

It's not over yet. That's the part she doesn't know. We're only getting started. Virgin or no, this was going to be a long night for her. I needed to take the edge off, needed to slake the smallest fraction of lust that I've felt for five years so that I could work her over good.

I leave her in a puddle of unsated lust to take care of the condom in the bathroom. When I come back, she's actually sitting up, smoothing her hair back from her face.

As if we're done.

A nudge with my foot to her inner thigh. She looks up, confusion in her brown eyes. If only I could warn her. *Find yourself a nice doctor to have missionary sex with the lights off.* It's too late for warnings. I kneel between her feet and make a home for myself. A tug of her ankle, and she topples over on the mat. I press my face between her legs and breathe deep. Salt and sex and woman. I want to drown here. I lick her through the damp fabric of her leotard.

"I want you wet every time you wear this," I mutter, biting at the inside of her leg. "It's going to be so fucking embarrassing, having a wet spot between your legs every time you dance. Doing the splits and knowing everyone can smell how aroused you are."

She moans something that sounds like protest but feels like surrender.

"All the men in their suits. They'll pull out their dicks right there in the theater, watching you spin for them, watching you dance like it's your goddamn art, and all they want is a piece of this pussy."

Her hips jerk, and I hold her down, licking hard through the fabric, using my tongue and my teeth. It will never be enough friction with the leotard between us, and she keens her dissatisfaction with the barrier.

"The women would all be jealous of you, of this tight little body, of the way their husbands pretend to be interested in dance so they can imagine fucking you." Finally, finally I push aside the leotard. She's burning hot and so wet, the scent of her stronger now. "They want to be the ones onstage, instead of you."

Bethany rocks her hips in silent plea. "Josh."

"It's okay," I reassure her, soothing her clit with an almost-chaste kiss. "You can come."

I follow that up with a swipe of my tongue, and she comes with small, hard waves, her whole body clenched, her fingers tight in my closely cropped hair.

When she's done, she collapses again on the mat, but I don't let her have a moment. Instead I clamp my lips around her clit and suck. A high-pitched squeal fills the gym, but that only makes me suck harder. Her hands claw uselessly at my hair, pulling it, yanking it from my scalp, but it does not fucking matter. I work her body until she comes again, right on the heels of the last orgasm, her whole body bucking against me, a hoarse scream bouncing off the mats.

My lips are slick with her desire. She keeps shivering, her body out of her control now. It's under my control, and now she understands that. "You said—" She breaks off in a helpless moan. "You said you'd stop."

"Did you tell me no?" I offer an innocent shrug. "I don't think you did."

She's shivering and shaking, as if her body

can't decide what to do. I gather her in my arms and press a kiss to her cheek. "Close your eyes," I murmur. "Rest a moment. We don't have to hurry through this. We have all night."

Then her eyes do fly open. "All night?"

"You didn't think I was finished with you, did you? Under the circumstances."—*such as the fact that you were a fucking* virgin—"I won't ride you anytime soon. There's no help for it. I'm going to have to use your mouth extra to make up for it, though."

Her chocolate eyes are wide now. "I thought—"

"You thought one and done? No, ma'am. If you wanted someone without stamina, you should have slept with Landon. You let me into your body, and I'm real comfortable here. I'm a soldier first and foremost, and I'm not leaving until I know every inch of this terrain."

Still cradling her in my arms, I slide my right hand down her flat stomach to the bare skin of her cunt. She jerks away when I find her folds, but I'm persistent. A steady finger fuck brings her to inexorable orgasm, and she sobs in my arms as it takes her. "I know," I say, kissing her forehead. This is what she needed. It's what I needed, too. To hold her in my arms as she releases every dark thought. "Let it out. I'm here. You can trust me with this. You can fall apart."

I stroke her through the last of her climax. When she's done, I lick the desire off my fingers. My fingerprints are already wrinkled with the proof of her arousal. Gently I carry her down to the bed. She's sweaty and exhausted, and we're only getting started. I stroke my cock, which is ready for its turn again. I press the head to her lips. "Lick," I say, my body strung tight. I'm leaned over her like a predator, and I can reach her cunt with my right hand. "I'm going to come down your throat this time. And when you drink me, that's when I'll finally flick your clit and let you come again, too."

She doesn't tell me to stop. I knew she wouldn't. All we have is tonight, and I'm going to squeeze every drop of pleasure from her lithe body while I have the chance. I learned early in life that nothing lasts forever.

Sooner or later someone is going to leave.

Sooner or later that someone is me.

CHAPTER TWENTY

Misty Danielle Copeland is a ballet dancer for American Ballet Theatre, one of the leading classical ballet companies. In 2015, Copeland became the first African American woman to be promoted to principal dancer in the company's 75-year history.

BETHANY

IN MY DREAM there's warmth and grass and green eyes that sparkle with sensual promise. Sunlight brushes its thumb across my cheek. I stretch with my eyes closed, but instead of the plush earth, there's only silky sheets. Reaching my hand to the left, I feel for the solid body that should be there. The sheets are cool. My eyes fly open. I'm alone in the bed. Alone in the room. Maybe even alone in the house. Disappointment surges in my chest.

He's gone.

That ancient fear rises into the back of my throat. Maybe sex was all he wanted from me. My body at his beck and call. I pull the sheets over my head with a frustrated groan. I am too old for this fear to still be following me around like a vengeful ghost.

"Go away," I tell it, but it doesn't budge. I throw the sheets back. Josh's T-shirt flies out of the tangle and hits the floor next to the bed. Good enough for me.

I hear the clanging as soon as I step into the hall.

Josh is in his personal gym, one floor above me, lifting weights. I find him in the cramped space, the racks squeezed together, too close for comfort, because he moved them to make room for my dancing. Sweet relief. He's not gone. He's just involved in the manly pursuit of lifting heavy objects. For once I'm not the one being watched. I'm watching him as if he's on a stage. I lose myself in the way his muscles work. His bare skin glistens in the morning sun streaming through the windows. Joshua North is a hell of a sight, shirtless in his gym. I watch him unabashedly until he catches my eye in the mirror. A knowing smile moves across his face, and then it's back to concentration as he puts the weight in the rack and leans on the bench.

Standing behind him seems like the most

natural thing in the world, so I do it, skimming my hands along his shoulders and looking at him in the mirror. His eyes trace the line of his T-shirt against my thighs. He looks for a good long time, making me hot under the T-shirt. "I'm going to see your brother," he says.

The relief scatters like sidewalk chalk under a downpour. All that courage I gathered to find him here, and now this? "My brother?" It doesn't make sense. "That's what you were doing the night everything blew up before. You came back with blood on your clothes. On your face. And then you walked away from me." I can't stop my grip from tightening on his shoulders. I can't stop my nails from digging in. So I let go instead. "What the hell, Josh? Is that the future we're headed toward?"

"Of course not." He's so matter-of-fact that it pisses me off even more.

I take a step away from him, putting distance between us even in the mirror. "When are you going? I'm coming with you."

"No, you're not."

Oh, I hate how that firm tone makes me feel underneath all my anger. I hate how my body responds in spite of every single effort my mind makes. *Ignore it.* "Yes, I am."

"Absolutely not."

"He's my brother." I plant my feet and stand up tall.

"He's a traitor and a murderer."

My reflection flinches in the mirror, and heat skims across my cheeks. "He became a murderer because of me. That first time—he was protecting me."

He gives me a look in the mirror that makes me want to avert my eyes. He knows the truth now. He knows the full story. "That wasn't murder, and you know it. That was self-defense. That was putting down a rabid dog." Josh stands up from the weight bench and turns to face me. "I don't blame him for killing your father. That's one thing he did right in his life, but everything he's done since then? That's not on you. That's on him."

I'm standing here in bare feet and Josh's T-shirt, but that doesn't mean he's going to lecture me about my own brother. That doesn't mean he's going to forbid me from leaving his house. I lift my chin an inch. "If you respect me, then you have to take me with you."

The moment shimmers between us. My heart runs wild. I don't know what he's going to do. If he shakes his head, if he dismisses me, then this can't go on. None of it. I'll leave his mansion right now, and I won't come back. I rehearse my reaction in my head. No yelling. No tears. Just a cold acceptance, a quick turn on my heel—

"I agree."

"In that case—what?" One blink of my eyes and he's a different man. The Josh I knew five years ago never would have done this. He would have broken before he bent. He's changed. My lungs fill with sweet possibility. This feels momentous, and it is. It absolutely is.

He crosses the room so I can see his eyes with a crystal clarity. "I agree. You should come with me." But even in the afterglow of victory, I know that this isn't just about Josh growing up. It's also about fear. Fear for my safety, I realize when he leads me out of the gym at a fast clip. I saw it in his eyes.

JOSH

CALEB LIVES ON Frenchman Street in the Marigny, in a three-bedroom apartment on top of a famous tattoo shop. The fucking prick has been hiding in plain sight for years. I suppose he thinks that if he plays the part of a popular society man, people will forget about the fact that he's a murderer and betrays this country on a regular basis. Fucker.

I wouldn't come here if I had any other choice. But Caleb and I don't chat on the phone anymore. I have his address so North Security can keep tabs on him and step in if he tries any especially egregious bullshit. We let him run drugs, because I'm not the world's goddamn mommy. I stop him from dealing in weapons or humans, though.

He's not happy to see me when he opens the door to his apartment. I kick it open another foot before he can shut us out. "You really take the bolt off the chain without checking the hole? You're going to get killed making stupid mistakes like that."

"Fuck you," he says.

"That's original." I keep up the running commentary while we stroll in the front door. Caleb scowls at the both of us, standing back with his arm sarcastically extended to usher us in. He pushes the door shut not a second too soon.

"What do you want, North?"

"Heard from Connor lately?" I stretch arms above my head, which has the intended effect of reminding Caleb about the gun I keep tucked in my waistband for occasions like this.

"No." Caleb's eyes flick toward the ceiling. The fucker still has the balls to roll his eyes at me. "You made sure of that."

"I'm only checking because Connor's been harassing your sister. You should see the threats he sends her in the mail. Really choice stuff." For the first time Caleb's eyes slide to Bethany. She faces him head-on, arms crossed over her chest.

"Is that true?" His voice has a shake to it I recognize. It's abject fury.

Bethany nods.

Caleb looks back at me. "And what the fuck are you doing hanging around her? I've got people to watch her for when she needs protection."

"Well, they've been doing a shit job, since one of the letters got hand delivered to her locker. And you don't appear to have heard about any of this. Admit it, Caleb. Was it Connor? Are you two having a little fun, like in the old days?"

Caleb stabs a finger at my face. "You don't have the right. You don't have the fucking right to be anywhere near her, you piece of—"

"This is why we came here?" Bethany puts her hands on her hips. "So you could have yourselves a pissing contest in front of me? Are you serious?"

"I'm your brother," Caleb says with a growl.

"You're domineering." She glares at me. "So

are you. Both of you are bastards."

"No argument here, sweetheart." I give her a wink, mostly to annoy Caleb.

"Neither of you get to control me. Neither of you have any rights on me except what I agree to." Her dark eyes pin me to the wall. "And I have a performance."

Caleb doesn't want to blink first, and neither do I. We both let Bethany walk out the door. Noah's waiting in the car downstairs. He'll watch over her for a few minutes. We need to work something out, man to man. Bastard to bastard.

Her footsteps fade to nothing. Then it's just me and him.

"You fucking her?" he asks.

"Like she said, that's none of your business."

"She's my little sister. I protected her before you even knew she existed. Now you think you can take over because you have a goddamn Escalade and a government contract? I know what you really want."

I step forward, putting my face an inch away from his. This is the language that bullies understand. It's the language that I speak more fluently than English. "Because I want your sister's pussy? Yeah. You didn't need Mamere's crystal ball to figure that one out. So what are you going to do about it?"

A vein pulses in his forehead. "I can kill you. I can *ruin* you. I can—"

"You can stop running your mouth for a goddamn second, and answer a question. Before you puff up your chest anymore, know this: your sister's safety is at stake. Have you had any contact with Connor?"

A tense moment. "He came at me six months ago. Said he'd just gotten out of lockup, had this crazy idea it was my fault, said I owed him something."

"Funny how ratting out your friends pisses them off."

Black eyes flash with hatred. "You're one to talk."

"That's where you're wrong. You and I? We were never friends. You wanted to use me, but I used you first. Now tell me where Connor is."

"I don't fucking know. He didn't exactly leave his business card."

"Think."

"I don't know! He looked high as fuck, and I gave him some money so he'd calm down. That's all. I gave him some money because I felt sorry for him."

I'd love to keep pushing, pushing, pushing

until Caleb lets loose with something more helpful. Unfortunately, I think he's telling the truth. At the very least he'd offer to sell out his so-called friend for money if he had a line. Plus he seems genuinely pissed off at the idea of anyone—me, Connor, or goddamn Captain America—touching his sister. He's always treated her like she was six years old.

"He contacts you again, you call me."

A sudden laugh that seems almost boyish. "He contacts me again, he's a dead man. And I wouldn't make any long-term plans if I were you, North. No one who messes with Bethany gets away with it. That's a promise."

CHAPTER TWENTY-ONE

A teacher from Bakersfield, California, played the video game 'Just Dance 2015' for 138 hours 34 seconds, earning herself a world record and raising over seven-thousand dollars for charity on the live stream.

BETHANY

MY PIECE-OF-SHIT APARTMENT is exactly the same as I left it.

Josh was wrong. Nobody cares enough to break in.

I had him drop me here instead of the theater because the rest of my performance clothes are still hung up over the kitchen sink, drying for weeks now. I've been at his place too long. He offered to buy replacements, but I didn't want that. He's not going to give me another thing. Not today. I wrench the clothes off the hooks and shove them into my messenger bag.

I don't know how I'm going to get over that

ridiculous visit to my brother's place. I don't need to see him at his house. We cross paths at Mamere's and that's enough for both of us. Ugh, this apartment is baking. My windows have been closed—for *security*—and I'm sweating inside five minutes. It's disgusting here. I hate how much I'd rather be at Josh's mansion. I hate how much I'd rather be with Josh.

Instead it's Noah who brings me to the theater and back. Noah who brought me to my apartment so I can grab some more clothes. Noah waiting in the front of the building.

How does Josh spend a night like that with me and go right back to fighting with my brother? As if I'm some piece of meat to be fought over? I take the final step onto the cracked concrete sidewalk, still fuming.

And look up to find an empty curb.

No Noah. No black SUV. No sign of him at either end of the street. Shit.

This is rule number one of staying safe—be aware of your surroundings. I wheel around, heading back for the door. "Uh-oh," says a voice behind me. It almost sounds kindly, like I've dropped a receipt from my purse and someone wants to give it back.

By the time I've turned fully around, I know

exactly how wrong I am.

I'd know Connor anywhere. He hasn't changed. Except that his grin has gotten more screwed up by the year. It sends a wash of cold to the pit of my stomach. "Hey, Connor," I say tentatively. We never spent much time together. Not until I needed some money. Not until—

"Where's your guy?" He shrugs his shoulders, that grin plastered on his face like a mask. "Somebody's supposed to be here to pick you up. Your brother's always got his people lurking around, but I don't see them." He taps the side of his cheek, an exaggerated mockery of thinking. "Oh! I know. They got tangled up with the North asshole's man. They can all have a little party. I bet someone else will be here to pick you up."

I hesitate. The hesitation costs me everything.

Connor's gotten faster, and I haven't been practicing sprints. He catches me around the throat after a single step. My whole body jerks back as if I've run into an invisible wall. "I know who's here to give you a ride, sweetheart. It's me."

JOSH

A BABY KICKS in its stroller, jostling the array of fabric and plastic insects hanging above him.

Another child drags his mother toward the bright candy-filled shelves of the newspaper store. Disinfectant and Starbucks coffee scent the stale air.

I've never met anyone at the airport before. What's the point?

Even when I reconnected with my brothers, we were all self-sufficient enough to find our own way home. Somehow I got roped into meeting Liam and Samantha. They're fully capable of driving themselves to their hotel, but here I am. It feels strange, like something a family would do. Liam, me, Elijah—we were more like a nuclear wasteland than a family.

Somewhere along the way that changed.

Maybe it was when Liam fell for Samantha. Maybe it was when she got pregnant. The bump is barely noticeable, but Liam acts like she's made of fucking glass. The idea of a child would terrify me, but he seems happy.

Happy. The idea is foreign.

It's not meant for men like me. Or is it? Bethany's been staying with me for weeks now, and I don't feel stifled or trapped. I like her in my bed.

The thought of her leaving makes me feel something close to panic.

A text appears on my phone. North Security's

private jet has landed safely. It will only take a few minutes to complete the airport's procedures, so I push through the sliding glass doors. I watch the jet come to a rolling stop. The stairs fold down and Liam appears at the top. He helps Samantha down, who's carrying her violin case. That much hasn't changed.

When I reach them, I give Liam a quick hand-clasp. That's as close as we've ever come to caring physical contact—and a far cry from the punches and kicks our father used on us. Samantha isn't shy. She throws her arms around my neck, and I hug her back, feeling uncommonly emotional. "What's up, squirt?"

She gives me a gentle shove in retaliation. "What's up is that I'm glad to see you. Where's Bethany? I'm so glad we could make it before her show ends."

"She's in practice, but you'll be able to see her tonight."

A sly look falls over Samantha's expression. "Oh, that's right. Because she's staying with you. And here I thought you two didn't like each other."

Discomfort moves through my stomach. I don't want Samantha playing matchmaker. Then again, it's not like she needs to. I've settled

Bethany into my life pretty well on my own. Settled her so deep I can't imagine living without her. "For safety reasons."

Liam frowns. "Have you made progress on her stalker?"

"Some." Not as much as I'd like.

My phone vibrates on my hip. I lift the screen to see a phone call from Noah. My blood runs cold. Why would he be calling me? He's supposed to be picking Bethany up from the theater right now. He'll bring her back to my place, where she's safe, safe, safe.

Time slows as I press the green button on my phone. "North."

Noah sounds unsteady and far away. "They got the drop on me."

A visceral sensation, like something being torn apart—internal organs ripping to shreds. That seems more likely than the idea that Bethany's in trouble. "What do you mean?"

"Some men were sniffing around. Caleb's people."

"They took her?" There's a clench in my chest where I hope that's the answer. Her brother's fucking crazy, but he doesn't want her hurt. If he has her, I can get her back. She'll be okay. *I need her to be okay.*

240

"They insisted I walk away. I refused." In those few words I know that my friend must be really fucking injured. "When I tried to call for backup, a third guy came from behind. I was fighting the three of them when she came out of her apartment. He was ready. Waiting. He must have known these fuckers were going to make a play for her today. It was exactly the distraction he needed."

My blood runs cold. "Connor James. He has her?"

My eyes meet Liam's, and I suddenly understand every insane thing he did to save Samantha, every pillow he puts around her pregnant body, every moment of soul-deep fear when she might be in pain. Is this love? It feels like death.

"Affirmative."

CHAPTER TWENTY-TWO

Tupac Shakur is best known as a rapper from the late 80s and early 90s. However, he also studied ballet and poetry at the Baltimore School of The Arts. He played the Mouse King in their production of the Nutcracker.

BETHANY

JOSH. HE'S THE first thought in my head. His green eyes, playful and merciless, demanding that I get it together. Pain pierces my head, and I fight against the tides of unconsciousness pulling me down.

It would be so much nicer in blind and blissful ignorance.

There wouldn't be this ache or this dread.

Instead I lift my head. It's dark, and my eyes can capture only dust motes and shadow. Then slowly, the expanse of a room. Pictures flash through my mind in close succession, a horror reel of my afternoon—my apartment, the black

SUV.

Where's Noah? Has something happened to him?

Well. Something must have happened. I remember the sound of Connor's laugh, like a deranged frat boy. Something small and black in his hand. And then the most terrible pain searing my nerves. A taser? Jesus.

There's something very menacing about a taser. It shows a level of forethought that chills me to the bone. It's almost worse that it's not a gun—it means he doesn't want to kill me. No, he wants to drag this out. He wants me under his control, and he doesn't care how much it hurts.

There's humming somewhere in this cavernous space.

It echoes off the walls, slightly out of tune and broken up, raising goosebumps on my arms. It's the Dance of the Swans. Which could be random, but considering Landon adapted it from Swan Lake for his show, Duckling, it feels pointed.

As if he knows that.

As if he's been watching me even when I've been rehearsing.

Footsteps cross the floor with a familiar sound. This isn't a regular floor. It isn't concrete or tile. It's parquet, the same kind we used to practice. I blink up at the ceiling. It's mottled and moldy, but it looks familiar, too. Where did he take me? Lingering pain still clouds my senses.

Someone looms over me. He kneels. "You're awake, little dancer. I've been waiting for this performance for a long time. You don't even know how long, do you?"

The unhinged lilt in his voice makes me shiver. "Connor?"

"You remember me. God, I was worried you wouldn't. But I didn't need to be."

I wonder if I should stroke his ego. I wonder if that would keep me alive longer. A fist squeezes my heart, because I want to see Joshua. I want him to hold me, except I never should have let myself fall for him. Not five years ago. Not today. "Of course I remember you. You worked with my brother."

Immediately I know it's the wrong thing to say. His expression turns dark, almost feral. "Your fucking brother. He sold me out for his freedom and a bottle of Jack. Him and Josh got real cozy."

My breath catches. Connor blames my brother. That's fair enough. It's more scary that he blames Josh. Will he go after him next? "It was a long time ago."

A short laugh. "Five years seems like a long

time when you're behind bars. Even that was lucky. I had to turn over so much fucking information for them to even meet with me. Name after name. Detail after fucking detail until we could finally make a goddamn deal."

"I'm sorry," I whisper, and strangely enough, it's true. Connor deserves to be behind bars. He probably deserves worse than that. Except I wanted my brother alive. I felt that much loyalty to him. So I asked Josh to help, and despite his cruel words, he did.

In a complex way, I'm responsible for what happened to Connor.

A blunt finger traces along my jaw. "Don't be. You're going to make it up to me. I've been dreaming of you. Imagining you dancing. All those times Caleb wanted me to walk you home, as if he didn't know I'd want to fuck you. He wanted us to see what we couldn't have."

The shadows behind him finally sharpen, and I suck in a breath. We're in my old dance studio. The last time I was in here, Josh was the one who escorted me home. Soon after that everything came to a head—and when Caleb lost his source of income, I lost the ability to pay for these lessons. I kept dancing, of course. I made my own way in the world, without the help of my brother or his terrible money. "Connor." I try to make my voice sound reasonable, as if we're having a conversation in Starbucks instead of with my hands tied behind my back. "I understand you're upset with Caleb. And with me. You have a right to be angry, but I—"

"With you? No. No, I'm not angry at you." He makes an abrupt movement with his hand, as if cutting off his hands. "I know I sent those letters. Maybe I was angry that you hadn't visited me in prison, but I understood. Your brother wouldn't let you."

I stare at him, a cold chill settling over me. It sounds like he's created this story of a romance between us, one that I should have pursued, one that I wanted. "I didn't know you were in jail. I didn't know that, but even if I did, I wouldn't have visited you, Connor. We barely knew each other."

His brown eyes narrow. "You little bitch."

Part of me knows I should placate him. He's the one with the taser—and probably worse weapons. The other part of me is truly offended by the very idea of placating him. "We can get to know each other," I say, throwing out the idea more with panic than any real plan. "I want to know about you."

He's not fooled. He might be crazy, but he's not exactly dumb. He wouldn't have been useful to Caleb if he couldn't see through a blatant lie. "Enough talking. That's not what I was dreaming about all those years behind bars, anyway. I was thinking about this." He runs a hand down my side, cupping my breast through my clothes, and I gasp out, "Stop."

A hard smile. He squeezes my breast until tears prick my eyes.

"You're going to dance for me. The best performance of your life, aren't you? You make me enjoy it, or I'll make you regret it." His erection looks large in his sweatpants, and I feel like I might throw up. Mamere always said that being a dancer was no different than stripping. I always said she was wrong, but here in this moment it's like the nightmare's come true.

JOSH

THE LAWS OF man evaporate. Red lights mean nothing. Drivers blare their horns. I don't care. *I don't care.* Bethany is the only thing that matters on the face of the earth. This is what she does to me. This is why I had to walk away from her five years ago. She turns me into this frantic, hungry, gaping hole of a human. I don't care if the whole world explodes, as long as she's safe. She's kryptonite to me, and I'm dying.

I've had a twenty-four hour-watch on Caleb and Mamere. That's how I know he didn't take her to the apartment on Marigny or to her old house. We get Landon on the line, but no one there has heard from her at the theater. Where is she right now? *Where, where, where.*

My dark heart beats the question a million times a minute.

Think, I tell myself. *If you were a sick fuck, where would you take her?*

It's not that hard to imagine. The line that separates me from a sociopath snakes like a babbling brook through my consciousness. At the moment there's a drought. If I were stalking Bethany, if I really wanted to have her, really *own* her, where would I bring her? No, I'm asking the wrong question.

Caleb and Noah and I, we've grown up. For better or for worse.

Connor got put away. That was part of the deal that Caleb struck. He turned over his accomplices in exchange for freedom. Connor's been in jail, rotting away, mostly the same as he was five years ago.

If the old me were stalking Bethany, where would I go?

The answer comes to me in a blur of sunlight and the loamy soil of a cemetery. Her brother practically paid us to stalk her under the guise of protection. We watched her run down the concrete steps. She dashed across the street in her leotard and sweatpants. To want Bethany is to want her dancing. They're one in the same.

What better place to watch her dance than at her old dance school?

The space sits above a cigar shop that's closed for the day, wrought-iron shutters thrown over the windows. I'll burn this fucking place to the ground with him in it if anything happens. My chest seizes at the thought. Fuck. I can't even think about it. There's no time to think. There's only time to throw myself out of the car. The damn thing's barely in park. I leave the door open and run, my pulse a rolling thunder.

Access to the warehouse is around the back through a shitty plywood door. He's locked it. Connor has locked the fucking thing. A thousand doors made of steel and concrete couldn't keep me from her now. I put my shoulder into it. The building shudders. A dull pain on the second try. It barely penetrates my fury.

The door splinters, cracking in the center.

A sliver juts out and cuts through the fabric of my coat on the third hit. Blood. Pain. They don't matter. I knock it off its hinges and step over the broken remains.

A narrow staircase. A thick layer of dust.

And the sound of Bethany crying.

Red clouds my vision. It's bloodlust, as pure as I've ever felt it. I storm the stairs, gun in my hand. Safety off. Whatever he's done, he's going to pay for it. I was the devil's son. Now I'm a goddamn avenging angel. The steps bow under my weight. This place is a relic of the past. It's barely holding on. *Hold on, Bethany. I'm almost there.*

The final step brings the scene into sight.

Bethany, tied to the barre with a thick belt. A length of leather around each wrist. It's a perversion of something that could be so sexy. But he's not giving her pleasure. No. He's meting out pain, twisting her body like she's some kind of doll.

Connor has a foot on her upper back, arching her spine forward in an unnatural curve. She can't get her arms loose. What the fuck is his plan? To kill her like this? To snap her neck with the heel of his shoe?

His eyes are bright with insanity. She's like some kind of doll in a mad music box, and he thinks he can twist and twist the little knob to make her dance. *How dare he touch her?* I'm just as crazy as Caleb, because I think I have a right to her body, the right to protect her.

I take aim. Time slows. *Squeeze.*

I put a bullet in his forehead. Red sprays in a small, futile refusal. The shot echoes. Bethany screams. Connor falls in a rain of blood.

He falls away from her. Thank fucking God.

She's sobbing when I fall to my knees next to her. The belts come apart in my hands, freeing one hand, then the other. Bethany falls forward into me, gasping for air.

I feel her for injuries, my heart pounding. Any moment I'm going to find it—the fatal gash, the handle of the knife, the slick opening of a gunshot. But there's nothing, other than two bruised circles around her wrists and a raw circle between her shoulder blades from that fucker's shoe.

I'm afraid to move her. Afraid that if I stand up, everything will shift into something dire and unrecoverable. The blood soaking into my pant leg from Connor's body is what finally spurs me to my feet, Bethany in my arms.

She squeezes her eyes tight.

"You're okay," I tell her. I offer it as a prayer all the way down the stairs and out to the car. To the other cars. Somehow, Liam is here too, all our people surrounding us. Someone drives us back to my place. My pulse doesn't begin to slow until the two of us are behind my locked door.

Hot showers. Fresh clothes. Bethany is silent and heavy-lidded. "You're okay," I tell her again, and lower her gently into my bed.

I've never wanted anything more than I want to climb in next to her. But I pull the covers up tight, sealing myself out. I go back to my place on the sofa. All I can do now is stand guard. Connor's dead, but that doesn't mean there are no other threats lurking outside. For today, at least, and tonight, I'm keeping watch.

Maybe forever.

"What are you doing out here?"

"I'm where I need to be." The words escape without thought. "Someone has to be out here to protect you. I have to be out here."

"You need to be in the bedroom." Despite what she's been through, every step is light, graceful. Weightless. "Next to me." Bethany comes to stand in front of me. She nudges her hip against my knees. She forces her way in close. "In the bed. This is the sofa. You need to be in the bed," she says in a soft chant. "The bed. With me." Every word is a puncture in the distance I'm trying to keep between us.

She takes my hands in hers. "I can't do that." I'm so fucking tired. My life has been exhausting, and it's spilled over in this moment. I thought loving her would crush me before. Now it's grinding my bones to nothing.

Loving her made me weak. Now it's made me dust.

"Yes, you can. Look at me." I do. God, she's beautiful. And bruised. Because I couldn't protect her. "There's nothing between here and the bed but an open door."

"I know."

"And you still think you can't go in there with me?"

My instinct is to hold her hands tight enough to crush them. The reality of her forces me to be gentle. At least in this moment it does. "Do you know what it did to me when I found out he had you?" The feeling rushes back. Sickening. The air goes out of my lungs. "I was so fucking afraid. It ruined me."

"You came anyway," she says. "Connor's dead. I'm safe."

"You're safe for now." The pain is so great, the fear so strong. The threat to me so real, more than bombs or guns. I can't have her. I can't even be near her. "For now. And I would do anything to keep you safe."

Only because I can't survive the alternative.

Even in love I'm a selfish bastard.

Bethany rubs her thumb into the sensitive inside curve of my hand. "Is this the same fight as before?" A wry smile softens her face. "You're afraid you'd do anything for me?" She looks down at our joined hands. "That it would be too much of a risk for a man like you?"

"No. What's left to risk? I'm already lost." I bury my fingers in her hair, bringing her eyes back to mine. "How the fuck will I ever live without you?"

One heartbeat and she climbs into my lap, straddling me. Her muscles are sure and strong. Her hands might be small, but they're steady on the sides of my face. Bethany kisses the corner of my mouth. She grazes my bottom lip. Her gaze is surprisingly steady. I almost can't meet her gaze, but I force myself to do it. "You don't have to live without me." With one knuckle, she taps against my breastbone. "Choose to live with me. Right now. Choose it. I won't take no for an answer."

Under her kiss the fear flies away, replaced with a low, burning desire. I kiss her hard. Harder. "That's my line, sweetheart."

I let her mouth soothe me, even as my desire rages higher. Nothing is solved, though, because no one's ever really safe. She'll always have a crazy brother. She'll always have unhinged fans. How the fuck will I ever live without her?

I wasn't lying before. She ruined me. I'm gone.

BETHANY

THE FIRST THING I'm aware of in the morning is the emptiness. I've slept here enough nights to know when I've got the whole bed to myself, and I do.

Josh should be here. I can still feel the mark of him all over me.

He covered what Connor tried to do with gentle kisses. Then he fucked it out of me. He took my pleasure into his own hands, and now all I can feel is him. The horror of those hours in the dance studio are already fading. It won't be long before I can let myself believe it was only a nightmare.

Wispy, like the suggestion of ghosts at a séance.

Not even there.

I was mistaken before, when I thought the sheets smelled like him. Now they do. I breathe him in. This is what home smells like. What safety smells like.

A shadow falls over the bed. I open my eyes.

Josh stands at the side, fully dressed. A pressed suit. Not one errant wrinkle. He's ready for…work? He looks down at me, his expression impassive.

The sun falls around him like a halo. This man is no angel. "Morning, sweetheart." He reaches down and rubs a thumb roughly over my cheek. "You want a ride? I'd do it myself, but I have a meeting. Noah can escort you home."

Dread tightens my stomach. "What?"

"You didn't think we were going to play house, did you? Christ, I can see the answer on your face. That's embarrassing. Look, we caught the guy. You're safe now."

My cheeks are the same temperature as the sun. Tears prick the back of my eyes. What is he doing? "I don't understand."

"Let me spell it out for you. You were a nice fuck. Now it's over."

"Bastard," I say, barely able to squeeze out the

word.

"You won't hear me deny it."

"Why are you saying this stuff to me?"

"Because it's true."

The words ring… false. They hurt me, a fresh cut oozing blood from an old, deep wound. Even knowing he's full of shit, he can hurt me. I push myself upright on the bed. "You don't mean that. I don't know why you're doing this, but I know you care about me."

"Of course I care about you. I don't want you dead. I don't want you to be some crazy fucker's little ballerina doll. I care about all women that way. That doesn't mean we're going to ride off into the sunset together."

A flinch. "Stop it."

"Stop what?" His voice is taunting.

"It's natural to be scared. Everyone feels like that sometimes." I feel like a PBS special, but it's the truth. And I get the impression Josh could have used better childhood programming. We both could have. I reach for his hand.

He pulls away. "You know, I thought that might be the case. But when I woke up this morning, I realized that everything is still the same. You're just not worth that kind of investment. No pussy is."

Goddamn. Like I'm a piece of property in a business deal. He's doing this on purpose, and I won't stand for it. I won't let him hurt me like this again.

Not when I know the truth.

I grit my teeth. "You're lying."

"Am I? I meant it back then, and I mean it now. Same as ever." I see it, deep behind the green of his eyes. A flicker. A flash. Like distant heat lightning. I want to yank the storm out of him. I want to stand in it with him and let him see how it can't really touch us. But he turns away, striding for the door. "Noah will drop you off at your place. Let him know if you need transportation in the future. He probably wouldn't turn down a fuck for a few favors."

Every word out of his mouth feels like a knife in my body. There's a dull throb from the attack yesterday. Everything hurts, but nothing as badly as his cold look. I force myself to kneel on the bed, pulling the sheet around me like it's a robe, like I'm a queen instead of a broken ballerina. "Josh. I know you're afraid. I'm afraid, too, but I love you. You want to push me away? Fine. Consider me pushed, but I know the truth. I love you, and I think you love me, and you're breaking my heart."

His head cocks to the side like I've said something curious. Maybe something in a foreign language that he doesn't understand. "I don't love you," he says.

I flinch. I'm not going to crumple in front of him. Not this time. "Maybe. But maybe you do love me. Maybe you just have to let yourself love me. Would you?" God, he could end this pain. He could end it right now. I've been here before. I don't want to be here again. But I'd rather be here with him than anywhere else in the world. "Would you let yourself be this vulnerable?"

He blinks at me. And for one horrible moment I allow myself to hope.

Joshua North shakes his head.

No.

It's more than an answer to my question. It's a refusal of everything. Of me. Of us. Of love. It's the last thing he does before he leaves the room, this man who's saved me a thousand times, this man who won't let me save him back. It's not the violence that scares him. It never has been. It's the certainty that he'll lose me, that he'll lose everyone. He'd rather walk away before it happens. He's the bravest man I know, but in this, in love, he's still a goddamn coward.

CHAPTER TWENTY-THREE

"Those who were seen dancing were thought to be insane by those who could not hear the music." –
Friedrich Nietzsche

JOSH

BUYING A TICKET to Bethany's last show at the box office feels more illicit than an arms deal. It feels dirtier than double-crossing a man I thought was supposed to be a brother-in-arms. It feels like I'm the world's biggest scumbag, and a stalker on top of that. Which is accurate.

I am being a fucking stalker. There's a certain level of guilt that comes with that, but not nearly enough to make me stop. In fact what I'm really struggling with is the urge to find Bethany in her dressing room, throw her over my shoulder, and hide her away forever. What I'm doing is bad, but what I want to do is worse.

I behave myself because I can pretend to be a gentleman under the right circumstances. I won't fuck up her last show, no matter how badly I want to. Liam and Samantha have front row seats to the final show. They're somewhere in the sea of people. Above us, in one of the boxes, is her brother and his entourage. He's still a crazy fucker, but he does actually care about his sister.

Me? I'm in the back row. From here I can see everything. I can feel everything.

And it's not what I expected.

Honestly I thought I was coming here to assuage my own guilt over being a piece of shit. I'm not dumb enough to think I didn't break her heart. I know I did. It was written all over her face. Let's not forget that I have prior experience in the matter. I know exactly what I did. Tonight was supposed to be proof that she still had something to love in her life, even if I wasn't worthy of her heart.

The performance gives me a sinking feeling.

Bethany moves under the lights like she always has. Effortlessly. In defiance of gravity. She spins and lifts and bends her body in ways that I always thought were an expression of deep joy. But I was too fucking blinded by lust to look at her face. I'm looking now. The smile locked into place is fake. It's for show. For the patrons. It's the same one she was wearing when I caught her delivering the glass of champagne to that douchebag in the lobby.

Nobody around me has any idea.

They ooh and aah and clap and gasp. A woman to my left catches me staring, grim and horrified. They have no idea. They think this is all real. That she loves putting herself on display for their entertainment. That she wants nothing more than to be seen as a body in motion. It's not much better than Connor tying her to the barre with his belt. It's fucking sick.

The standing ovation takes me by surprise.

I'm not prepared for the song to end. I've been too disheartened by this new version of Bethany. I can see right through her facade. Jesus, she's good. I believed it. I fell for it hook, line, and sinker. What the hell does that say about me? Nothing good.

Nothing has ever been good about me, and this is no exception.

When she takes her final bow, I wipe my hands against my jacket. My skin feels dirty just watching this. I'm garbage, just like the rest of these people. Worse. Because I bought the ticket to make myself feel better, when she's the one who's empty. No joy on her face. No joy in her heart. She's just doing Landon's bidding. It has nothing to do with her. Even when the crowd gets on their feet for a standing ovation, Bethany wears the same blank smile.

Fucking heartbreaking.

I'm ready to escape, several steps down the aisle, when the lights go back down. What the hell? The audience doesn't know what to do with this. "What are they doing?" an old woman to my right says in a tremulous voice. "Is there an encore?"

Marlena takes center stage then, a portable mic in her hand. I didn't recognize her in the ensemble without her sultry attitude. She puts on a hint of it now while she speaks into the mic. "Good evening."

Those two words are enough of a cue for everyone to take their seats. Everyone who's interested, anyway. Some people—assholes—file out through the side doors and let them shut loudly behind them.

"We've prepared a special finale." Marlena's voice is smooth. Unafraid.

Landon looms in the wings on stage right. He looks fucking furious. So it was a surprise for him, too. Good. Marlena does something to the bottom of the mic and flies on tiptoe to intercept him. She drags him back into the shadows.

A single beam of light lands on the stage. Bethany's there, her head bowed.

She's changed out of her costume and into a simple black leotard and pale pink tights. It's the costume a child would wear for ballet class, but no one could mistake her body for a child's. For a moment she stands perfectly still.

My heart trips over several empty beats.

The music comes in. One. Two. Three. A different beat. Something dark and fast, like a river at night. Like the molten core at the center of the earth.

Bethany comes alive. I've never seen her dance like this. Not once. These steps—they're something totally new. But I recognize them as intimately as I'd recognize her skin under the palms of my hands or the roll of her hips when she comes. I've felt this every time we've ever touched.

It's the essence of her. The power of her.

Her performance fills the room. The music in the air and the sound of her skin connecting with the stage are the only things I can hear. All other noise is irrelevant.

All other people are irrelevant.

I'm entranced by her. Consumed with her. The real her. This woman. This queen. When the music stops, its echo ringing through the auditorium, I'm the first to my feet. She might never know I was here. I might never have the chance to tell her. So I clap until my hands feel raw, until my throat feels tight with emotion, and then I clap some more. In this moment I'm not anyone special. I'm just a man who loves her—like every other man in this room. Every other woman. We're all in her thrall. We're all her subjects as she gives us a simple, elegant curtsy and exits the stage.

BETHANY

THE OLD SWING behind Mamere's house should probably be torn down. It's creaky and rusted over, but it can still bear weight. There's a lesson in there, if I cared to learn anything from all of this.

There'll be time to learn later. When my heart comes back to life.

If it comes back to life.

Even if it does, I know it won't beat the same.

"A sorry sight, you here alone on that swing. Not even the spirits to keep you company." Mamere shades her eyes against the setting sun. "Does it help?"

"To swing?" I try to imagine a set of circumstances that would be helped by sitting on a derelict swing. None of them look quite like the one I'm in. I finally got to show the world the dance of my soul. It was beautiful and heartbreaking, because I had no one to share it with. A theater full of people. *Alone.* "No, Mamere. It doesn't."

The breeze runs its fingers through my hair and pats my cheek, as if New Orleans is comforting me. Not completely alone. I have Mamere. I have the city. I have dance. What I don't have is the man I love, because he'll never let me in.

Not five years ago. And not now.

No more, Bethany. No more hoping he'll come back. No more wishing for pebbles against my window. All that is done. Someday I'll feel peace about that. There will be wise words about serendipity and the vagaries of the heart.

Someday isn't today.

Mamere shuffles through the tall grass and grips my shoulder. I put my hand over hers, feeling the papery skin and the tendons in sharp relief. She's always been this way, ethereal and so very real. We stand that way for a long time, my toes pressed into the grass, my gaze on the pink-orange sherbet sunset.

Then she releases me and goes back into the house. I lift my feet from the ground to let the swing move again. Back and forth. Back and forth. The creaks become a sort of music. They mark a slow and steady rhythm.

There's beauty in everything, even heartbreak.

I once sat on this swing as a terrified little girl. Then I grew up into a scared young woman. I'm not afraid anymore, and I wouldn't go back to what I was—not even for the man I love. He's too afraid to be vulnerable; that's the irony of strong men.

The wind stills. A presence makes the hair on the back of my neck rise. My heart pounds faster. I couldn't say what changes, whether I feel the bend of the grass or the shift in the air. It could be anyone. It could be no one. My soul whispers: *Josh.*

I know better than to hope for that. Don't I?

My breath catches. I turn around to prove myself wrong.

The sunset provides a saturated spotlight. Peach light limns his tanned skin. It skates over the stubble on his jaw. It turns away from heavy shadows on the angles of his face. Objectively I know he's a handsome man. Rugged and masculine. My heart jumps into my throat. I'm not objective. He doesn't look handsome to me; he looks like fire.

How did I think I could swing and swing and swing?

How did I think living without him was an option?

"Josh. You're here." I stand, abrupt and clumsy, without an ounce of my dancer's grace. The swing doesn't want to let go. One of the rusty chains scrapes against my palm, leaving a thin line of blood. I hiss, more surprise than pain, but I barely glance at it. I'm transfixed by the man standing in the yard, the light trapped in his emerald eyes.

He closes the distance between us with his long strides and takes my hand in his. He turns it over, and I'm struck by the memory of reading his palm. He's reading mine—not the lines in my skin. He's reading the pinpricks of blood. His eyes flick up to meet mine, and a shock both foreign and familiar ripples through me.

"You're going to need a tetanus shot," he says, his voice grim.

A wild laugh tears from my throat. The sound floats above us on the breeze. Josh cracks a smile. "Is that all you have to tell me?"

"There were a few other things. They can

wait."

Such practical ideas—bandages and Neosporin. I have no desire to walk through those rituals. I have no interest in the lines on my palm. They don't decide my fate. That's in the hands of a man with violence and anger and unspeakable tenderness. *He came back.* "You walked away from me, Josh."

"I'm an asshole."

That makes me smile. "I know."

He glances away. A muscle ticks in his jaw. "That probably won't change anytime soon. Not at the core of me. Even if I—"

"Do you think you're telling me something I don't know?"

"Christ."

"You've been living in this space a long time," I say, understanding Mamere's words more than before. "Haven't you? Very much alone." He stands like the tower against a starless sky. The tower means danger. It means upheaval.

It means destruction.

He drops to his knees, all six feet plus of him.

The tower, falling. Or maybe a better word would be dismantled. He's choosing to bring it down. For me? Or for himself? They might be the same thing. I feel the impact through the soles of my feet. My non-bloody hand slips easily through his hair. I tilt his face up so I can see his eyes.

"I came here to tell you that I'm a bastard. That I'm sorry for everything I said. For everything I didn't say. Most of all I'm sorry that I didn't have a front row seat at the finale, because you were a goddamn goddess."

It feels like my heart's expanding. Overflowing. "You were there?"

"I wouldn't have missed it. I'm too selfish to miss it."

A watery laugh. "You're trying to convince me to forgive you?"

"No. God, no. In the history of time. In the history of humanity. There has never been a bigger bastard than me." He turns my bloodied hand over and brushes his lips against my knuckles. "Don't ever forgive me."

He's kneeling in front of me like I'm a queen. Like he's a knight. That's what we are, in a way. I can point in a direction; he's the one who fights. "What if I want to forgive you?" I don't mention that it was already done. Forgiveness isn't really a decision. It's threaded with love and trust. It's his whether he wants it or not.

"You really shouldn't."

"What should I do instead then?"

He holds my hips with two large hands, almost enveloping me. He rests his forehead against my sternum. "Start with a tetanus shot."

I press a kiss to the top of his head. "I forgive you."

"Don't."

"And I love you. That's never been a question."

"I'm not sure I can take it." His voice is unsteady, and I know that he's telling the truth. Blood and guns and treason. That's the language he speaks. Forgiveness is a foreign word. It's beyond anything. *It's everything.*

"Do you love me, Joshua North?" Blood races through my veins. I know the truth, and maybe that's enough. It's not. It's not enough unless he can admit it. He needs a woman strong enough to forgive him. I need a man strong enough to ask for it. "That's the only way this works. Do you?"

His hands tighten on my hips, as if he can feel me slipping away. "I love your loyal heart. Even if you forgive more than you should. I love your beautiful body. Even though the world doesn't fucking deserve your talent."

I tug on his arm, and he stands. "What do you love?"

"I love you." His green eyes burn with unspoken pain.

"You love me, even though…"

"Even though it kills me. It kills me to need you."

"Same," I whisper, putting my hand on his chest. His heart thuds against my palm. We were both in towers, both so bent on destruction in order to be safe. I feel that seismic shift as I look into his eyes—the foundation beneath my feet cracking, the endless fall. This is what it feels like to fall in love. It isn't a moment. It's forever.

CHAPTER TWENTY-FOUR

*Loie Fuller was a burlesque skirt dancer in the late
19th century who experimented with the effect that
gas lighting had on her silk costumes. She developed a
form of natural movement and improvisation
techniques that were used in conjunction with her
revolutionary lighting equipment and translucent
silk costumes.*

JOSH

IN MY DREAM there's a tower crumbled to
pieces.

I'm walking through the rubble, pulling aside
chunks of concrete, searching for someone.
Bethany. The name is enough to bring me back to
waking.

A dark room. Stillness.

I'm alone in bed. I know that before I open
my eyes, before I swing my arm across the cool
sheets on the other side. There's no surprise, only
a low throb of inevitability. Of course, of course.

Of course she left me.

It's an old wound, the way a broken bone aches in the winter months.

Being abandoned. Doing the abandoning.

Both of those have left their scars in my body. I'll never fully escape them. The bone has healed, but the scar tissue will always be there.

Bethany won't abandon me.

I know she won't, because there's something stronger than muscle and weapons—there's love. I almost lost her a thousand times, but she's with me anyway. She's with me because she's strong enough for the both of us.

Knowing that she won't leave doesn't stop the dread in my body every time she's away. That's the thing about childhood pain. It sets in deep.

It never really goes away.

She could be having a cup of warm tea in the kitchen.

She could be practicing her new routine in the gym upstairs.

Instead I find her on the floor in the living room, a fire blazing in the hearth despite the warmth around us. I'm already feeling the heat as I sit cross legged opposite her. She has a deck of tarot in front of her, her hands resting lightly on her knees, eyes closed.

"Thought you didn't go in for that mumbo jumbo," I murmur, and my voice comes out hushed because there's a strange energy in the room. The same energy I feel in Mamere's house.

"Smoke and mirrors," she says, a smile playing at her lips.

"You've seen how the sausage gets made."

Her eyes open, and I'm looking into brown eyes that are a thousand years old, an eternity of wisdom. "That's the thing. I've seen people looking for comfort, for solace, for hope—and I've seen them finding it. There's a kind of magic in that, don't you think?"

There's magic in you. It sounds too sappy to say out loud, even for a man head over heels for a woman. Instead I gesture toward the deck between us. "Are you looking for hope?"

She raps her knuckle on the deck, and I know from what she's told me that she's clearing out the evil spirits from the cards. A gentle push and the deck is closer to me. "Are you?"

I look askance at the cards. I don't know if I believe in what they say, but I'm more concerned that Bethany believes it. What if the cards tell her to dump the bastard she's with? What if they warn her that I'm going to walk away? That's the crazy thing about abandonment. I can never be sure other people won't leave. I can never be sure that I won't leave, either. I don't trust anyone. Especially not myself. Her eyes glisten with understanding. "Shuffle them."

Love can make a man do crazy things. It can make him hope for a happily ever after. It can make him shuffle a worn deck of tarot cards. I do until she looks satisfied and set it back down on the floor between us. She asks me to cut the deck, and I do that, too. She could ask for anything. I'd follow this woman off a fucking cliff, so it's easy enough to make three piles and put them back together.

Her slender hand falls to the deck, almost protective the way she pauses. There's a shudder deep inside me, a fear that she'll pull that same card—The Tower. That it will prove I'm meant to be alone. So much destruction. That's all my life has ever been. I tried to destroy Bethany, too, with cruel words and cruel actions, but she was too strong to break.

The Chariot. A man in armor stands tall in a chariot, two lions ready to pull.

She taps the card with her forefinger. "This is a card for a warrior. It's about determination and action and success. It's almost the exact opposite of The Tower."

"I'll tell my brother," I say, because he's been hounding me about getting back to work. Of all people he knows what it's like to find love, he knows the obsession that comes with it, but North Security has more business than it can handle. I'm staying with Bethany until she stops having nightmares about Connor. And then maybe I'll stay longer. I'll stay fucking forever.

"There are stars in the curtains. Moons on his crescent. This is not just a card of physicality. It's about finding success inside you, not accidentally, but with pure willpower."

"Willpower." An interesting way to describe love. The right word for someone who was burned early and often in life. It took determination to decide to work for it again. To fight for it again. To risk everything on one little dancer who stole my heart the very first time I saw her spin and leap in a derelict warehouse.

BETHANY

I TRY NOT to wake him up. In my dreams it's not Josh standing behind Mamere's house. It's Connor, who never even visited there. It's my brother, who's in the city committing crime. It's my father, who once read bedtime stories. Before he decided I looked too much like my mother. Before he drank too much to tell the difference between us. At six years old I learned not to trust anyone.

It took a lifetime to learn to trust again.

I stack the tarot deck again. "I'm sorry I woke you up."

He gives me a baleful look. "You didn't."

Of all people, of all men, I learned to trust Joshua North. He's a self proclaimed bastard, an injured animal biting anyone who comes close. *Auribus teneo lupum.* I have this particular wolf by the ears, which means I'm going to get bitten— and I'm choosing not to let go. "I tried to be quiet, but you always hear me anyway."

"I told you to wake me up when that happens."

"What's the point of both of us being awake?"

"The point is that you shouldn't have to be afraid alone."

My heart squeezes. "I hate that he can still affect me like this."

As I say the words I'm not even sure whether I'm talking about Connor or my brother. Or my father. I hate that fear can still emerge when I'm sleeping, when I'm helpless to keep the dark images at bay.

"A bullet was too fucking quick. I want to kill him again."

I squeeze my eyes closed. Not fast enough. A tear escapes down my cheek. "He wanted me to dance for him, and I could have just—I could have just done it, you know? I've danced for thousands of people. But I couldn't do it. Not like that."

A low growl from my wolf. "Of course not."

"And I keep thinking... what if he broke me? What if I can't dance for anyone? Not just on stage, but dancing someone else's steps? That's my job, but more than that, it's what I'm good at, the only thing I'm good at. What if I've lost that?"

"Then you'll dance for yourself."

"The dance company—"

"That fuckface director doesn't deserve you. No one does, actually, but that's beside the point. You dance what you want, when you want to, and if anyone says otherwise, I'll ride my fucking chariot over them."

I have to laugh at that, despite the heavy weight of my nightmare, despite my serious worry about my future. There's no doubt in my mind that Josh would fight any battle I want him to. If anything I'll probably be holding him back. "You know, Mamere always said that dancing was no better than being a stripper."

"Listen, your grandmother's batshit crazy. And I'll put up with her crystal ball and her incense and her random predictions, but I'm not going to put up with her saying anything about you. If she says that in front of me I'm going to have some words."

Lightness suffuses my chest. "How do you do this to me, Joshua North? How do you make everything feel possible?"

He cups my cheek in a rough palm. That's the only warning I have before he's kissing me, his lips demanding entrance, his movements urgent. "Everything is possible," he murmurs, his mouth against mine. "You forgive me. You love me. How can anything be impossible knowing that?"

That's how I know I'll dance again. Love is the hardest thing. Forgiveness. He's right about that. If those things are possible, then everything is.

He bears me down on the carpet, muttering to himself about the stars and the moon. Something about a chariot as he pulls the clothes from my body. The fire dances heat across my bare skin. It's nothing compared to the emerald fire in his eyes. I look down, unashamed in my nakedness. There's nothing to be afraid of when he's full of raw need. My legs open for him, a clasp for his muscled thighs. He pulls back to press himself into me. We're combined in the most elemental way. We're forged in fire in front of that hearth, as bright as the stars. We move together, ocean waves pulled by the moon, salt licking at the sand. In that moment of blinding heat, we find forever.

EPILOGUE

*In the tarot deck, the World card depicts a woman
wearing only a cloth, dancing inside a large laurel
wreath. She looks behind her to the past, while her
body moves toward the future.*

BETHANY

THE LIGHTS FLICKER three times, meaning the
show is about to begin.

Through the heavy velvet curtain I can hear
the shuffling of expensive wool and silk as three
hundred guests take their seats for opening night.
They turn the pages of glossy programs that
feature my photo in black and white.

"Nervous?" Marlena sparkles in a white costume with crystals.

She's everything pale and shimmery tonight.
There's something elemental about dancing in a
plain leotard, the way I did on the finale. This is
our debut as a new dance company. Reporters
from nineteen different outlets, both local and

national, have press passes. We have full costumes and a gorgeous set designed by a husband and wife team of artists. The entire warehouse has been transformed into a night sky with dark netting and fairy lights. It's like a grown up blanket fort.

"So nervous," I confess. "My hands are shaking."

She grins. "That's a good thing. It means you're alive."

I laugh a little unsteady. "Then count me extra alive. Times a hundred."

"We're going to blow their freaking socks off."

"You are, that's for sure." Marlena shines as the figurative crystal ball, the fountain from which our dancer spirits appear. They spill out from her in artistic display, both demons and angels, called forth to the earth through her body.

My own costume has just as many sparkles, maybe more. Except these are midnight blue. Swarovski crystals shaped like stars and crescents cover my torso. A skirt made of patchwork silks in purple, blue, and green rounds out the picture. I'm the quintessential fortune teller, the classic New Orleans psychic. I'm Mamere. In the dance I'll consult my crystal ball, searching for answers—and I'll find them in the form of tempestuous spirits. Some of them are moaning, others are mischievous. They pull at my skirt and my sanity until I question what's real.

It was time to branch out on me own. I realized that after the attack. I suppose I knew that for a while, but as I fought with myself—my pride, my dignity, my struggle to survive—under Connor's hand, I became sure of it. Marlena came with me, along with a sizable endowment from Scott Castle for us to launch the new dance troupe.

I peek from between the dark curtain.

Green eyes watch me steadily.

Josh knows I'm back here pacing, because I've been pacing for days now, weeks even. I've been worried, but he hasn't been. *You were made to do this,* he says.

Only right now it feels like I was made to throw up.

I give Marlena a kiss on her cheek, partly comfort that I need, partly gratitude for her coming with me. "You're going to be amazing."

A playful smile. "I know. Scott's going to be so hot for it tonight."

"You two are crazy."

"As if you aren't getting plenty of action."

Action. Yes. Joshua North is a man of action.

That's why he brought me to the warehouse, blindfolded, to show me how he had a platform installed. It was only the beginning of an idea, the barest bones, but it was everything I needed.

We've renovated the space, but there's still an industrial feel. The lack of mercy these four walls have seen. I like a little dark history. It tempers the brightness of the day. "Am I insane for starting my own dance company?"

We're a little late in the game to have second thoughts. I've already formed a company and an advisory board. I already have the goddamn business cards. "Yeah," she says, looking exhilarated. "I love that about you."

The truth is I feel exhilarated, too.

Soft notes skate over the air. It's our cue to get into place.

Marlena steps forward to the center of the stage, curling in on herself. Later she'll stand and dance. For now she's an inanimate object. Even the spirits slumber on various parts of the stage. I'm the only one standing as the curtains slide open.

In the front row I see Josh's brilliant green eyes. In the distance I see his brother Liam and Samantha. I can even see my brother's figure lounging in the back with his entourage. There's only one person I'm focused on, one person who understands.

And when I leap into the air, it's him I'm leaping toward.

Thank you so much for reading Josh and Bethany's book!

If you haven't read OVERTURE yet, don't miss Liam's story…

Liam North got custody of the violin prodigy six years ago. She's all grown up now, but he still treats her like a child. No matter how much he wants her.

"Swoon-worthy, forbidden, and sexy, Liam North is my new obsession."

— New York Times bestselling author
Claire Contreras

"Overture is a beautiful composition of forbidden love and undeniable desire. Skye has crafted a gripping, sensual, and intense story that left me breathless"

— USA Today bestselling author
Nikki Sloane

Sign up for the VIP Reader List to find out when

I have a new book release:
www.skyewarren.com/newsletter

And if you enjoyed this emotional second-chance romance, you'll love Before She Was Mine by Amelia Wilde. *I was never allowed to love Summer Sullivan. I loved her anyway. And then I took her heart in my hands and crushed it.* Read BEFORE SHE WAS MINE now >

Join my Facebook group, Skye Warren's Dark Room, for exclusive giveaways and sneak peeks of future books. Turn the page for an excerpt from Overture…

EXCERPT FROM OVERTURE

*R*EST, LIAM TOLD me.

He's right about a lot of things. Maybe he's right about this. I climb onto the cool pink sheets, hoping that a nap will suddenly make me content with this quiet little life.

Even though I know it won't.

Besides, I'm too wired to actually sleep. The white lace coverlet is both delicate and comfy. It's actually what I would have picked out for myself, except I didn't pick it out. I've been incapable of picking anything, of choosing anything, of deciding anything as part of some deep-seated fear that I'll be abandoned.

The coverlet, like everything else in my life, simply appeared.

And the person responsible for its appearance? Liam North.

I climb under the blanket and stare at the ceiling. My body feels overly warm, but it still feels good to be tucked into the blankets. The blankets he picked out for me.

It's really so wrong to think of him in a sexual way. He's my guardian, literally. Legally. And he has never done anything to make me think he sees me in a sexual way.

This is it. This is the answer.

I don't need to go skinny dipping in the lake down the hill. Thinking about Liam North in a sexual way is my fast car. My parachute out of a plane.

My eyes squeeze shut.

That's all it takes to see Liam's stern expression, those fathomless green eyes and the glint of dark blond whiskers that are always there by late afternoon. And then there's the way he touched me. My forehead, sure, but it's more than he's done before. That broad palm on my sensitive skin.

My thighs press together. They want something between them, and I give them a pillow. Even the way I masturbate is small and timid, never making a sound, barely moving at all, but I can't change it now. I can't moan or throw back my head even for the sake of rebellion.

But I can push my hips against the pillow, rocking my whole body as I imagine Liam doing more than touching my forehead. He would trail his hand down my cheek, my neck, my shoulder.

Repressed. I'm so repressed it's hard to imagine more than that.

I make myself do it, make myself trail my hand down between my breasts, where it's warm and velvety soft, where I imagine Liam would know exactly how to touch me.

You're so beautiful, he would say. Your breasts are perfect.

Because Imaginary Liam wouldn't care about big breasts. He would like them small and soft with pale nipples. That would be the absolute perfect pair of breasts for him.

And he would probably do something obscene and rude. Like lick them.

My hips press against the pillow, almost pushing it down to the mattress, rocking and rocking. There's not anything sexy or graceful about what I'm doing. It's pure instinct. Pure need.

The beginning of a climax wraps itself around me. Claws sink into my skin. There's almost certain death, and I'm fighting, fighting, fighting for it with the pillow clenched hard.

"Oh fuck."

The words come soft enough someone else might not hear them. They're more exhalation of breath, the consonants a faint break in the sound.

I have excellent hearing. Ridiculous, crazy good hearing that had me tuning instruments before I could ride a bike.

My eyes snap open, and there's Liam, standing there, frozen. Those green eyes locked on mine. His body clenched tight only three feet away from me. He doesn't come closer, but he doesn't leave.

Orgasm breaks me apart, and I cry out in surprise and denial and relief. "Liam."

It goes on and on, the terrible pleasure of it. The wrenching embarrassment of coming while looking into the eyes of the man who raised me for the past six years.

Want to read more? Overture is available on Amazon, iBooks, Barnes & Noble, and other book retailers!

BOOKS BY SKYE WARREN

Endgame trilogy & Masterpiece duet

The Pawn

The Knight

The Castle

The King

The Queen

Trust Fund duet

Survival of the Richest

The Evolution of Man

Underground series

Rough

Hard

Fierce

Wild

Dirty

Secret

Sweet

Deep

Stripped series

Tough Love

Love the Way You Lie

Better When It Hurts

Even Better

Pretty When You Cry

Caught for Christmas

Hold You Against Me

To the Ends of the Earth

Standalone Books

Wanderlust

On the Way Home

Beauty and the Beast

Anti Hero

Escort

For a complete listing of Skye Warren books, visit

www.skyewarren.com/books

About Skye Warren

Skye Warren is the New York Times bestselling author of dangerous romance such as the Endgame trilogy. Her books have been featured in Jezebel, Buzzfeed, USA Today Happily Ever After, Glamour, and Elle Magazine. She makes her home in Texas with her loving family, sweet dogs, and evil cat.

Sign up for Skye's newsletter:
www.skyewarren.com/newsletter

Like Skye Warren on Facebook:
facebook.com/skyewarren

Join Skye Warren's Dark Room reader group:
skyewarren.com/darkroom

Follow Skye Warren on Instagram:
instagram.com/skyewarrenbooks

Visit Skye's website for her current booklist:
www.skyewarren.com

ABOUT AMELIA WILDE

Amelia Wilde wrote her first story when she was six years old, a narrative strongly inspired by The Polar Express. When she was nine she wrote her first novel-length work, all in one paragraph.

Now, Amelia is all about that love. Her romances feature unique, independent heroines and alpha heroes who are strong of heart and body. Readers have described her work as "emotional," "intense," "phenomenal," and "like a child scribbled with a crayon," which she takes as the highest praise.

Like Amelia Wilde on Facebook:
facebook.com/skyewarren

Join the Let's Get Wilde reader group:
facebook.com/groups/letsgetwilde

Follow Amelia Wilde on Instagram:
instagram.com/awilderomance

Visit Amelia's website for her current booklist:
awilderomance.com

Copyright

CPSIA information can be obtained
at www.ICGtesting.com
Printed in the USA
BVHW031706220223
659023BV00001B/74